TO CRY A DRY TEAR

Bill MacPhee's journey of hope and recovery with schizophrenia

BILL MACPHEE
WITH
JOHN MOWAT

iUniverse LLC
Bloomington

TO CRY A DRY TEAR
BILL MACPHEE'S JOURNEY OF HOPE AND
RECOVERY WITH SCHIZOPHRENIA

iUniverse books may be ordered through booksellers or by contacting:

iUniverse
1663 Liberty Drive
Bloomington, IN 47403
www.iuniverse.com
1-800-Authors (1-800-288-4677)

Because of the dynamic nature of the Internet, any web addresses or links contained in this book may have changed since publication and may no longer be valid. The views expressed in this work are solely those of the author and do not necessarily reflect the views of the publisher, and the publisher hereby disclaims any responsibility for them.

Any people depicted in stock imagery provided by Thinkstock are models, and such images are being used for illustrative purposes only. Certain stock imagery © Thinkstock.

ISBN: 978-1-4917-2271-8 (sc)
ISBN: 978-1-4917-2272-5 (e)

Printed in the United States of America.

iUniverse rev. date: 2/11/2014

CONTENTS

Brick walls, cold and white.

Heart pounding. I'm scared. Why am I here? How can I get out?

Distinct smells assault my nostrils.

Arrows pointing this way and that.

Are those arrows there for me? Am I the only one who can see
them? Are they there for me to follow, to give me direction?

Numbers on the walls, lighting up.

Are they a code? What are they trying to tell me?

I am in a wheelchair, cold steel pressing against me.

Racing down the wide hall.

Urgency - nurses' voices shout at the other patients to stay in their rooms.

One tells me everything is going to be OK, trying
to sooth me with her comforting voice.

Voices in my head tell me she lies.

Four nurses pushing the chair crowd me.

Arrows, they point the way out for me. I must escape.

A man at the end of the hall, dressed in white. Everyone in white.

An orderly. He is evil, I can tell. I can sense it. He looks
normal, but I see he's evil because he isn't handsome.

I must get out. I must escape.

The exit in front of me, blocked by the orderly, the evil orderly.

Leaping out of the wheelchair. Running, coming up fast on the
orderly. Move right, so does he. Move left, so does he.

I scream, "Get out of my way."

I swing. A connection. His evil face is contorted, blood
gushes from his mouth, stains his white uniform.

I turn and cry in rage. Something crashes. People are yelling.

I must get out.

Confusion. Fear. Why was I brought here? Someone
must know. Why won't they tell me?

Bright lights pin me in their glare. Blind.

Is this my resurrection? Is that why they brought me here?

I have to get out. I'm filled with an awful dread. Did He feel this?

Retrace my steps, past the nurses.

They scatter to make way for me. Nothing can stop me.
Run, get out. Its all a blur. They fear me, I can't be stopped.
Curious faces peer anxiously behind locked doors.
"Get him!" "Restrain him!" The voices yell.
Footsteps pound behind me, running, chasing me.
I see freedom, is this a dream?
Hands on my shoulders, around my neck.
I can't stand, going down.
"Get the needle"
What needle?
So many hands holding me down as I fight for freedom.
*   I struggle desperately like an animal in a trap.*
The drugs take over, I have no strength.
Relaxing. I can't fight any more. I tried.
Dragging me towards a room. What's in there?
Blackness. Sleep.
Awake. How many hours have passed? How long have
*   I been here? It seems like seconds or days?*
A bed. A strap across my chest. Shackles, thick blue plastic
*   shackles on my wrists and ankles. Too tight.*
Calmer now. Confused. Maybe this is resurrection.
Soon someone will come to tell me what is going on.
The door opens. Two people walk into my room. They
*   look at me curiously. They're not dressed*
like doctors. Jeans, regular clothes. Who are they?
Is this one Cassie?
It doesn't look like her. Maybe she was brought into
*   the hospital to be resurrected as well.*
Is this my new body?
Am I Adam and is she Eve?
I reach out to touch her. I want to touch her. I want to caress her breasts.
Relief. She is here with me now.

CHAPTER 1

INVINCIBLE

Looking down I see the water swirling and racing by thirty feet below. It looks menacing and dangerous, ready to suck me to the bottom of the Niagara River, yet it is an inviting challenge to a young daredevil. This water calls to me with a familiar voice, like an old friend. I've made this jump hundreds of times. The sun is hot and the steel bridge will burn my feet if I stay in one spot too long. I do the usual hop from foot to foot. I'm constantly checking to see if there is a train coming, or maybe a patrol officer from CN Rail to chase me off the bridge that connects Fort Erie, Ontario, Canada to Buffalo, New York. Neither the notion of danger nor any thought of safety enter my head. I'm focused on the fun we're having.

My name is Bill MacPhee. I am thirteen and am trying to decide if I am going to jump or dive into the Niagara River on this hot, sunny July afternoon. Its 1976 and it doesn't really matter what I decide. I've made this trip head first or feet first many times before. I feel no fear. The water is inviting, refreshing and deep and kids like me have been jumping off this bridge forever. Of course there's an unlimited amount of teenage bravado operating to focus our attention. There's no thought of danger, nor any possibility of "chickening out." We all do this. My boyhood friends and I think we're invincible as we climb higher and higher on the bridge.

This is it! One giant leap forward – no turning back. There is the feeling of nothingness beneath my feet. I'm falling through the air, hearing it rush past my ears. The wind blows through my hair. For a moment I'm dancing in space. Freedom. There's nothing like the excitement these fleeting seconds bring.

The adrenaline surges as I plunge beneath the water and am carried off by the swift current. The hundredth jump is the same as the first – yet the thrill is forever unique.

Holding my breath and closing my eyes I feel the sudden cold shock through my body as I splash down into the emerald liquid of the fast flowing river. My heart jumps as it has countless times before. I kick my legs feverishly. Up, up and finally I break the surface. I let out a gasp and breathe fresh air. From burning heat to freezing cold, it's been seconds.

Wow! That was fun! It was just as much fun every time before and every time after. This is life for a young man in Fort Erie.

The current carries me and two of my friends, Steve and Mike, down river quickly past the same familiar scenes - the coal docks, Steve's house, the big yellow rock, and Willy's dock. All are easily accessible stopping points if we want to get out of the water. Where will we land this time? Usually we get out at Steve's house, but occasionally we let the water carry us as far as five miles downriver before deciding we've had enough.

Jumping off the bridge was one of our favourite summer activities. We tried to be the first ones into the river each year around the 24th of May, not long after the last of the ice floes from Lake Erie had made their way down the river to their final plunge over the falls, a twenty kilometer journey. It was an important matter of personal pride – to be first. After our daring attempt at bravery, we'd run, teeth chattering, with symptoms of hypothermia into Steve's house to warm up. Some years later Mike wouldn't come in the water that early.

"Chicken! Cluck, cluck, cluck! Mike's a chicken!" We would taunt and tease. Not me. I had no fear. Relatives and friends would exclaim, "You swim where? Where did you say you jump? When was that?"

Little did I know my lack of fear was establishing patterns in my life that would influence every part in the years to come. This personal characteristic would often get me into trouble later in life, but would also eventually be my saving grace and my greatest success. Perhaps it was as simple as the physical action of stepping off the ledge into the air that shaped my way of thinking for the rest of my life. Fear and danger became my friends. Somehow I would always be finding myself on ledges with thin air beckoning me forward.

I had a normal childhood, at least I believed it was normal. I thought every boy did the things I did.

Swimming was the love of my life! I grew up playing in the river. Fishing, water skiing and swimming. I wasn't supposed to jump off the bridge, but that never stopped me. From my early years Mom would walk me to swimming lessons at the Kinsman Pool in the morning, sit on the bench and watch my lesson, then back again in the afternoon for public swimming. I was at home in the water like I was born with fins and gills. I always had a great time, but it was never as much fun as jumping off the train bridge. It was probably the danger of it all, the fact that it scared my mother half to death and the possibility of getting caught and into trouble that made us such daredevils. My river excursions started around age twelve. My cousin Kevin and I started going to the train bridge and coal docks. On special occasions Kevin's uncle, Boy Cook, took us to Bertie Bay on Lake Erie or to Black Creek, further downriver toward Niagara Falls. I also loved jumping from the Black Creek bridge into the Niagara River. But the train bridge was our favourite. From time to time the CNR police would run down the tracks on the bridge to shoo us off. They could never catch us, they were too slow. We'd just jump into the river (ending all cold water hesitation) and they'd leave us alone. I guess they never really cared much what happened to us – they never followed us on land, as we floated downstream, to arrest us or lecture us or take us home to our parents!

Floating down the river to Mike's house, we'd get out, teeth chattering, in search of other mischievous adventures. I recall one day we ventured over to a new house being built a couple of doors from Mike's. Not surprisingly we ignored the danger or trouble we could get in. There was a big roll of rebar and, of course, we took turns climbing on it to make it roll and spin. I fell backwards off it and when I went to get up discovered I couldn't move. I put my hand down and felt blood under me. I had fallen on the sharp end of the rebar and was transfixed with the steel embedded in my leg. Mike ran to get his Dad who came and gently freed my leg from the rebar. He took me to the hospital. I was scared he'd be mad at me but he wasn't. Mike's mom went and told my Mom what had happened. Later Mom told me she thought the lady was coming to tell her I'd drowned in the river, her greatest fear in those days. However, the doctor at the hospital cleaned out the puncture wound and patched me up just fine. I still have the scar to this day. I didn't get into any trouble this time. I guess Mom was glad I was okay. She probably was just relieved I hadn't drowned. I'm sure my adventures in those days didn't help my mother's already fragile mental health.

My Mom was scared all the time when we'd troop off with our water masks. She was sure one of us wouldn't come home one day.

Though I swam like I was born with fins, those fins didn't help me much when it came to school. I was an average student, and my teachers commented on my good behavior and attitude, but in general I didn't like school. I usually got Bs and Cs. Writing and spelling meant everything in those days and I was hopeless at both! My report cards always noted poor writing skills. I couldn't write neatly if my life depended on it. I tried holding the pen different ways, writing slower or using a different slant. It still all came out looking like chicken scratching! No matter what the teacher said, I could read my writing and that was the important thing – wasn't it?

"Billy, you have to do something about that penmanship. If you ever want to amount to anything, you need to be able to write." To this day my grade seven writing teacher's voice rings in my ears like a dull noise. In a dramatically ironic way, her negative attacks about my writing would become the force that drove me to succeed. I had to prove to her and the world that I could achieve. Later the written word would become the core of my personal and business life, bringing purpose and fulfillment far beyond any ideas I could have had then. I was born with a need to prove those around me didn't know the real me and I would show them my abilities by my success. It was like a sharp stick in the backside and I used it to propel me forward. I still do!

I did have some teachers I liked though. In kindergarten I had Mrs. Archer. I remember her kindness. She gave us towels to lie down on for our naps. In grade four I had Mrs. Thomas. When I met her years later she told me I was her best student. I'm not sure if she actually meant it or maybe she said that to all her former students and was just being nice to me!

I was quiet, obedient and respectful in school. Over time it became normal to just give me average marks automatically. I'm not sure if many teachers ever read my written work, probably because they couldn't! They'd just give me the average grade. I remember Mrs. Chow in grade six, Mr. Rosettani in grade seven as well as Mr. Abbys. I enjoyed all these teachers. I remember Mr. Walters. I liked him but he taught English, my worst subject. Since I was attending a Catholic school, I thought it odd that he wanted to talk about the racetrack all the time. In those days devout Christians didn't frequent the racetrack.

One teacher I didn't ever get along with was Sister Selema. She was the music teacher and I couldn't relate to music. In another of life's pleasant ironies, today my son Dwight plays the piano and guitar. I think this is a great gift he has and his teacher says he has an ear for music. He must have this gift from my wife Aileen. Not me, I used to play the triangle!

I went to a Catholic school from kindergarten to the eighth grade. When I was getting ready to go into grade nine, I wanted to go to Notre Dame College School in Welland with my friends, but my father wouldn't allow it. He said I'd have to mix with other kids eventually. The real reason was that Fort Erie Secondary School, where I ended up going, was free and Notre Dame cost money. We never had a lot of that. Even now when Dad has extra expenses at his nursing home he worries.

My parents never went to church or claimed to be religious, and to be honest, at the time I just went through the motions. I started attending St. Michael's Church at a young age. I became an altar boy and served at funerals, baptisms and weddings. I had my first Communion and Confirmation. I was the altar boy at my sister's wedding. I remember being terrified at Confirmation, praying that the Bishop wouldn't ask me a question. In the weekly services I was fearful when it was my turn to hold the reading for the priest, because I never knew when to turn the pages. It all seemed like the thing to do but I understood next to nothing. As I got older, I only went to church on holidays. In fact, I used to try to convince my friends to play baseball instead of going to church. I drank with my buddies but in my confession only admitted to my lack of attendance at church. That seemed a lot safer. I can remember my mother talking about giving to the church and getting back twice as much. I figured it must be some sort of financial plan. I had no faith and felt the church had no power. I wasn't even sure there was a God. But, as my father sometimes says, I was always a seeker.

I always loved my Dad and to this day hold high respect for him. But he did have his personal quirks. He was a no-nonsense father but he would spend a lot of time with us kids. His was a curious combination of strictness and fatherly involvement. If we wanted to go to the Sugar Bowl to play he would take us. The Sugar Bowl was and still is a giant park in the middle of Fort Erie. When the highway was constructed to the Peace Bridge, the construction crew mined gravel from this part of town and created a huge bowl in the earth. The town, with unusual creativity, turned it into a park with swings, a pond and other areas to explore. Dad would park the car and sit there reading his newspaper. We followed the paths and explored the forest that used to be there. Sometime later the Clemence family boys, friends of mine, got BB guns. We'd play war in the woods. I remember actually hearing pellets whiz by my head. Safety wasn't an issue for us. One time I caught Mike running down a path ahead of me. I hollered at him to stop and when he didn't I shot him in the back with my BB gun. Fortunately we never seriously hurt each other, no eyes were ever lost. Dad would beep the horn when he figured we'd been there long enough. On other occasions, he took us to the pump house at the river to swim and play in the sand. He'd bring his newspaper and read, but he was never one for sand castles. On weekends Dad played billiards. It was his hobby. He was a great pool player, the best in town, but he had an awful habit of swearing, particularly in the pool hall. I didn't like that. And everybody smoked in our house except me. Then it was just accepted as a habit. Life at home had its positives and negatives, like most other families I suppose.

Dad would take us to Helen's lunch restaurant on Gilmore Road once a week when Mom was in the hospital, it was a great treat. Mom was in the hospital a lot. With time she became a "stranger" to our family. We had a "family secret" that I didn't know till I was about eight. Our Mom had been married before and had three kids from that marriage. Tom, Cathy and Jack were my half siblings, and my father was Mom's second husband. This was a much bigger deal in those days than it is today. I respected my Dad because he adopted the other three kids and raised them as his own. Mom's first marriage was very difficult for her.

There was violence and abuse. I now have some understanding of the relation between mental illness and violence when a partner doesn't know. My mother suffered from manic depression and I didn't have much respect for her. She was always in the hospital. Now we know she was bipolar. Then she was just "sick" or "had breakdowns." At the time I didn't know either of those names. She'd accuse Dad of running around and was paranoid of our neighbors. I saw this as "weakness" at the time and was embarrassed for my dad. I constantly wondered, "Is Mom going to get sick again? Is she going to do or say something out of the ordinary?" One time in my teens I went to our family doctor and I questioned him, perhaps a bit too sharply. Mom underwent all kinds of blood tests and the doctor got the results but he could never tell us what was wrong or when she was getting sick. His reply was that they really didn't know and couldn't predict. I felt frustrated when this went on in our house. I told very few people of her hospitalizations, partly because I didn't understand what was happening and partly because I thought I was the only one who had a sick mother. At the time I saw her illness as a flaw in her character. Now when I talk to people I knew in high school, I find out I wasn't the only one with a sick parent after all. I wasn't the only one to think it was happening just in my family.

At a young age I probably knew the way from my house to the hospital better than the back of my hand. We'd make the trip every night when Mom was sick. Dad would leave me in the waiting room beside the wishing well, for hours while he was visiting Mom. Kids weren't allowed in the psych ward in those days. My wish was always the same – that my Mom would get better. She would be in hospital for three months at a time, only allowed home on weekends. On one occasion when she came home for the weekend, she couldn't keep still. She was up and down from her chair, cleaning house and pacing back and forth. We'd yell at her to sit still, read a book, watch television – anything. But she wouldn't or couldn't. When she went back to the hospital my Dad told the nurses what was going on. It turned out my Mom was on the wrong medication and that's why she was behaving that way. It made us feel pretty guilty.

Years later, as I lived through my own personal hell, I remembered Mom and wondered how she survived. My respect for her returned – I knew firsthand how difficult it is to battle mental illness.

Dad had average ambition. He started working in the shop at Horton CBI (Chicago Bridge and Iron) at age fifteen. He began as a "go-fer," and later moved to the office where he became a draftsman. He worked his way up to squad leader. This meant he supervised the other draftsmen and checked their work. He worked there twenty-nine years. I never got an allowance but Dad would give me money for movies on Friday nights. He was thrifty.

We never met any of my Dad's family – this was always a mystery to us. One day when I was about twelve a stranger knocked at our door when Mom and Dad were both out shopping. He said he was our grandfather and wanted to know if Dad was home. I found it odd when he didn't stay around and I told my parents when they came home. I don't recall any reaction from my Dad. Dad was very proud of his mother though. He sometimes would tell us about her. She was a great piano player and played for the silent movies at the Bellard Theatre on the Boulevard in Fort Erie. She became the first female customs officer at the Peace Bridge, a significant achievement in those days. Oddly, we never met her or visited her. Nor did she ever come to our house. To this day I still wonder just what went on in Dad's family to create this unspoken absence of his relatives from our lives. My Dad's grandfather was the first mayor of Bridgeburg, the old Fort Erie. Maybe our family was "famous," possibly for the wrong reasons and Dad wanted to shelter us from our background.

In our family of four kids, it was often my sister, Cathy, who is about nine years older than me, who filled in for Mom when she was sick. Around age twelve Cathy started to basically run the whole house. She kept the house neat and tidy, prepared meals and packed our lunches. One time it all "went to hell." Mom was really sick for a long time and

Cathy couldn't keep up with taking care of the family and the yard. The yard became a mess and we all were on pins and needles all the time. She loved to have fun too. One time at our parents' cottage in Muskoka, late at night when everyone was laughing and drinking around a campfire she and I dared each other to swim across the lake in the dark. We both took off our clothes and swam across to a neighbor's dock. At home Cathy was very popular. She belonged to a sorority in her high school years. Cathy and her friends would be in the basement and they used to call me down and say how cute I was. I thought I was the luckiest kid in town. I was about seven or eight at the time. Cathy was a great sister to me all those years. Later when she got married she moved to a house in Crescent Park, a subdivision in Fort Erie. Her husband worked midnights in a grocery store and she was afraid to stay home alone at night. I used to stay at her house to keep her company. I would joke that she was my favourite sister but she'd reply, "I'm your only sister." She lives around the corner from me now and we're still very close. We often take care of our Mom together at the nursing home, and she takes care of our Dad, making meals, and doing his laundry. I respected her and didn't cause her any problems when I was young. I still hold her in high esteem today.

Cathy

Mom went after Dad and me once. She thought we were out to attack her. She couldn't sleep at night. She was manic. She would vacuum at 3am and wake us all up. I recall one incident when I was in a sorority and we planned a bake sale. I wanted to bake cupcakes but Mom wouldn't let me. On the other hand when she was well, she was wonderful. We couldn't understand it. We had a great life. Her sickness came out of the blue. Mom would get sick and go out in her nightgown to the graveyard. The police would bring her back. If she went out for a walk she would peer into neighbors' windows. She often accused Dad of running around. When she was well Mom was there for her whole family. She would take dinner to our grandparents every night when she was well. She was a terrific person. I never discussed this with friends outside our home. Back then we didn't talk about this.

One time we took Mom to Hamilton for shock treatments. I went with Dad. It seemed the hospital staff blamed us for her illness. There were lots of locked doors. When we brought her home Mom looked like she was 100 years old. She was a mess. The psychiatrist put us through hell that day. I just smiled at Mom and that made him angry.

I often wondered why Dad stayed with her, he was so kind. Dad "hit" her only once. Dad had been through hell, she would leave at night. He didn't know what to do so he called the police. She had been harassing him all day. I remember lying awake at nights crying – it wasn't fair. What caused all this? We thought nobody else had this problem. Nobody talked about it. Grandma would say, "Don't tell anyone."

When Mom was well she was an excellent homemaker. She was proud of her house and liked it clean. It seemed, however, that around Christmas something would always happen. There would be an accident or Mom would get ill. She would say, "It doesn't seem like Christmas around here." It never did!

When Bill left for Singapore Mom was very upset. He was so far away. She worried about him every day. When Bill dated women in Singapore they were all "too dark" for Mom. But Mom immediately loved Aileen (Bill's future wife) when she met her!

Much of our family life revolved around Mom and her illness. It influenced and permeated every aspect as we grew up and into our adult lives. Dad was Mom's second husband. Dad married Mom when she had three kids and adopted us all. Dad was and still is special for what he's done and what he took on.

Bill

On the other hand, I never got along with my brother Jack. He is six years older than I am. It seemed he was always in trouble. He didn't care about school, so he always took special ed. He seemed to waste his life in my eyes. People said he had a "chip on his shoulder." He had "attitude." To this day he lives alone in subsidized housing. In my mind I mistakenly blamed him for Mom's sickness and her many hospital stays. She worried about him all the time and he caused her many heartaches. That part of my childhood was unpleasant and I was filled with hatred toward Jack. We'd always fight over the TV station. Today my disgust toward Jack is somewhat tempered by my understanding of the many challenges that accompany his situation. My parents would visit Jack in Welland and I would go with them. Once he got stabilized and out of the house he moved around a lot. He didn't get along with Dad and Dad told him he couldn't come back home. He was the author of his own difficulties and his own worst enemy. He was content to stay as he was, never making an effort to change.

I can now say with confidence in an ironic, negative sort of way, one of the reasons for my success today with my own family and our business is my brother Jack. I never wanted to turn out like him. His life has been a constant reminder to me and a key driving force for the measure of success I've achieved myself.

My other brother Tom is the oldest in the family. He is eleven years older than me and he made everybody proud. He was the perfect son in the family and star pupil at school. He was always the centre of attention and seemed to excel at whatever he attempted. I had great respect for him and always felt safe around him. He was an athlete, high school football star and became a policeman. At Christmas time he'd give great presents. One time he gave me a whirlybird helicopter and I thought it was the best present. He built his own bedroom in our basement. As close brothers like to do, we'd wrestle down there. It was great.

Sundays in our family always seemed to be a ritual when I was a kid. It was a day for most to sleep in, but I never did. Why waste a day by sleeping half of it away? I'd get up early and watch cartoons or play by myself – anything to keep busy. Sunday night was homework and bath night. It was also Ed Sullivan's really big "shooooow."

At the age of thirteen I got my first real job. I was a Dickee Dee ice cream boy. I took my position seriously. It was my first foray into the exciting and dangerous world of business and making money. I was a little young for the job, but I looked older since I was "big boned." At least that's what they called fat kids in those days. So I peddled around on a bicycle with a freezer attached to it, ringing my bell, selling barely-frozen ice cream during the long lazy summer days. It was a good experience learning to handle money, even in small amounts. I suppose the exercise and sweating helped me shed a few pounds too. At the end of my first day on the job, I got my initial hard lesson in business when my accounting didn't add up. I cursed the big kids for ripping me off. They'd do a planned raid – come at me six at a time. While I was serving one, the others took ice cream behind my back. Then when I tried to collect the payment, they'd deny they'd had any. They relied on the confusion factor – it often worked and I was left furious but helpless. I had to learn how to avoid places I might run into those guys. That job lasted two summers.

I have many good memories of growing up, especially of the Squires. This was the equivalent of a church youth group today. To join the Squires you had to be thirteen. In historic times, squires helped medieval knights dress for battle. We were the Junior Knights of Columbus so Squires was a fitting title. It was a great organization to be part of as a kid. We had weekly meetings and would play floor hockey or basketball. There was a chart and each member would get a certain amount of points for showing up at special events and meetings. We'd also work at the bingos held at the Fort Erie Race Track. We'd set up the tables Friday nights, then Sunday mornings we'd clean up the garbage and sweep the floors. It took us all day. We earned points for this work too. The point system was the way to qualify for the annual trip up north.

The trip took place every year around Christmas. It was a Catholic camp called Kumuntome. I can still see the cookhouse – it was a large building with a fireplace at one end and a huge wood-burning stove at the other. The camp had about five cabins, each big enough for six people to sleep. It was very cold but once the wood stove got started things would warm up and the flies would come to life and buzz around. I went on this trip four years in a row.

On one of our trips we went into Owen Sound for pizza and a movie at night. The priest, one of our supervisors, was called out of the theatre for a message that we found out later was bad news. Cabin rivalry and competitions were a huge tradition. Apparently some of the cabins had had a snowball fight and they had hung a blanket over a doorway to protect the fort. Due to their carelessness, the blanket had caught fire while we were away. It was too close to the stove. As a result the cabin burned to the ground. The kids from that cabin got sent home early! I was glad it wasn't my cabin.

The highlight of the camp, a daring midnight trek to a haunted house, took us through dark woods, over a lake, through deep snow, up a hill, through a field and over a barbed wire fence. This brought us to a road that led to the house. By this time we were all cold, soaked and thoroughly worn out. I remember walking up the driveway and feeling a frightening chill go through me. No Hollywood producer could ever make me as scared as that haunted house did. It was huge. If we weren't shivering and shaking from the wet and cold, we certainly were at the sight of that house. Three stories, broken windows and the corpse of an old rusted car next to the field gave us an eerie welcome in the dim light of the moon. There was an old well in the backyard that we were warned to keep away from.

About twelve of us frightened, shaking boys entered the house, all huddled tightly together like we were packed into a subway car. We walked up the stairs, broken floorboards all around and suddenly someone screamed. A ghost disguised as a dangling wire had brushed someone's shoulder. A door slammed in the wind and we ran back down the stairs in terror, but not before we gave at least one more thought to the coffin-like box in the basement. I'm sure everyone believed it housed a vampire who slumbered until it was time to greet the night and search for frightened boys.

Those were the good old days.

CHAPTER 2
WATER, DIVING and ASIA

I was a lifeguard at Crystal Beach when I was fifteen. You were supposed to be sixteen to be a lifeguard, so I lied about my age and I got the job. I'd achieved my bronze medallion at the Kinsman pool that year so in my mind I was fully qualified. I rode my bike out to Crystal Beach every day that summer for the job, a distance of twelve kilometres each way. For a guy who loved the water like I did, this was the ideal job.

I was compelled to learn more and explore the "pull" I felt from my interest in water sports so I decided I'd try to get my scuba license. I took lessons at the Kenmore YMCA near Buffalo, NY – eventually earning the Professional Association of Diving Instructors certificate. The instruction there was excellent and I progressed quickly. The excitement of learning to dive was marred by one negative incident that stands out in my memory and has never left me. It happened the week my parents went to Florida for a vacation. My brother Jack was supposed to give me a ride to my lesson but just before we were to leave he abruptly told me to cancel because he wasn't driving me! This was a cruel blow to me and he wouldn't have done it if our parents had been home. I called all my friends to find a ride, but to no avail. So I packed all my scuba stuff in a giant duffel bag and rode my bike across the Peace Bridge. It took me an hour and a half to get to the lesson! Later, when some others in the class heard I'd ridden all the way, I was offered a ride back to the Bridge. I was quick to take them up on the offer! This was just one in a long list of clashes with Jack. He and I were totally different. I seemed to have a deep personal drive to overcome adversity and accomplish things within my heart while he lived only for the moment, centered completely on himself.

I remember a girl, Maria, who was a daughter of the diving school owner whose name was, ironically, Bends. She was one of our teachers and a very experienced diver and swimmer. I admired her advanced skills maybe because I had a crush on her for a while. Years later I learned she drowned in the river, in a tragic accident at the same train bridge I had jumped from as a kid. I'm not sure if the possibility of drowning ever crossed our minds in those days – it was all boys' challenges and fearless bravado.

I was the only Canadian in the scuba course and they'd ask me about "that big statue over there." I told them it was Isaac Brock, the great British general. The statue, known as Brock's monument, stands tall and high in Queenston Park, several kilometers below Niagara Falls. At that time, it was the highest structure visible from the US side of the river. Apparently it never occurred to them we Canadians had heroes too. I didn't rub it in to them that he'd beaten the Americans in the War of 1812.

I joined the Fort Erie Underwater Recovery Unit at about age twenty-one. We'd practice our skills in the quarry at Sherkston, a nearby community. There was a sunken train at the bottom, making this an ideal place to learn. It was also the perfect place for discovery and adventure. Years before, workers were digging rock from the deep pit and had struck water. Overnight it flooded, trapping trucks, equipment and a train used to transport the rock to the surface. We would dive on this graveyard of machinery – it was great practice.

My love and respect for the water never wavered. Eventually I became a commercial diver working on oil rigs in the South China Sea and the

Formosa Straits. But to this day, the train bridge and Sherkston Quarry will always be my fondest memories of the water.

I had some wonderful friends in our unit – Jack Jordbane, Leonard Tate, Dan Baughn, Steve Simonds, and Don Burton to name a few. One of my fondest memories of this Recovery group involved Jack. He was a fellow diver who would tease me about my car – a Russian-built Lada. These vehicles were famous for never going far without breaking down. He would razz me mercilessly trying to make me feel guilty for buying a Russian car. I tried to explain to him it was all I could afford at the time. It was the cheapest car on the market. To my surprise many months later I noticed another Lada in the parking area for the divers. It turned out it was Jack's! The jokes and friendly taunting went both ways after that.

We'd go on dives and, of course, participate in the annual Niagara River raft race. Lots of clubs from Southern Ontario and Western New York came to compete in the event. It was a great day with floats and costumes highlighted by the race from Old Fort Erie near the mouth of the river to the train bridge, about five kilometers downstream. For many years the Fort Erie team won because we designed our "boat" for maximum speed. We used a ladder, attached to two-by-fours that held six giant inner tubes together. Six of us would get on this contraption, one in each tube and kick as hard as we could. We could move! These and other events were accompanied by parties and lots of fun times.

One year a group of us divers went to the US for a training session in Cattaraugus Creek. The current was very strong and while floating downstream we were suddenly surprised by a fallen tree branch stretched across in front of us. This was a very dangerous situation and we had come upon it without warning. I remember a few moments of panic and fear. Do I duck underneath and risk getting stuck or propel myself up and over the tree? In a split second decision I decided to go over, which turned out to be the better choice. I made it. Shoulder deep in the river, travelling with the swift current, I launched up like a dolphin clearing an obstacle, up and over the branch!

I see now why Mom always worried during these years. She'd say, "Don't do it – go have a nap." That was her solution for every situation! In those days I was different though – I needed the thrill of the risk deep in my soul.

My diving experiences eventually led me to go to Seneca College in Toronto, ON to take their Underwater Skills course. I started in 1981 and graduated a year later as a full commercial diver. I was eighteen years old. Part of the diving training was a welding course so I also had some welding skills when I graduated. The school had a pool with a forty-foot-deep hole in the middle. We did "hard hat" diving in this pool. They also had a lake – called Lake Seneca. We learned to dive in our lightweight KB4 helmets and suits. In the winter the lake was frozen, of course, but we'd dive anyway – in the freezing water under the ice. One task we had to learn was to assemble a gate valve underwater in the dark. I wasn't very good with my hands so could never get it done. It's a miracle I passed the course! I remember once I was diving in the lake and the job was to bury a pipe using a vacuum hose to suck sand for a trench. I noticed my breathing getting shallow, the air in my tank was getting low. I wanted to stay down longer so I opened my reserve tank – no air. I had forgotten it had already been used. I started to go up but the vacuum line had gotten tangled with my lifeline link to the surface, dragging me down instead. I dropped my weight belt and kicked hard for the surface, thinking the whole time "Mom was right, I'm going to die in the water!" I made it to the surface exhausted and had just enough strength to gasp "help me" to friends in the boat, then sank back under the water. Luckily, they dragged me in with my lifeline. I had blood in my mouth from drying out my lungs and had to go to the Toronto hospital. Nothing would stop me though, the next day I was back diving again and earned the great respect of my class for my determination.

When I graduated I wanted to work in diving and knew some guys from the course had gone to Singapore to work in Asia or the North Sea on oil rigs. One of the grads from the class ahead of us had gone to the North Sea and later died in a platform accident, one of the first accidents in the North Sea. He was killed in 1982 when the Ocean Ranger, the first oil rig of its kind designed to withstand extreme weather conditions capsized in a ferocious storm in the North Atlantic. All eighty-four crew on board died. I set my sights on Singapore, a decision probably based on my preference for warmer waters. I started working at Riches, a food manufacturing plant in Fort Erie, to save up some money. I went to the Toronto - Dominion Bank and told the manager, Bob Goodwill, my goals of working overseas and starting a diving career. My Dad co-signed for a loan of $2,000 for me to add to my savings to pursue my dream in Singapore. Over the years my father has supported my goals both in principle and with his finances. Once again he proved his support for me and his belief in me.

I got my passport and other paperwork together and on my nineteenth birthday boarded a plane to the east. It was 1981. I had no idea what was ahead, but was filled with lots of bright ideas and brimming with optimism. I have never stepped back from an adventure and was about to embark on a path that would influence my entire life. When we reached customs in Singapore I knew enough to say I was a tourist – not that I was looking for work. I checked into a nice hotel, thinking, of course, that the eastern world would welcome a bright, energetic Canadian like me with an immediate job offer. I was convinced I would land a great job right away. There were six dive companies in Singapore, three in the city, and three in the outskirts, an area called Jerong (the "silicon-valley" tech area of Singapore). The first day I went to the three companies in the city, the next day the other three in Jerong. During that first day, to my surprise I ran into some of my classmates from Seneca. Since they had been in Singapore for some time and knew the lay of the land to some extent, they directed me to move to the Mites Hotel which was a lot cheaper than the one I'd registered in when I landed. It turned out this was a very good move for a number of reasons. There were lots of us divers looking for work. We were friends and the companionship was appreciated by Canadian boys far from home, but it was like actors auditioning for a show. We never told anybody else if we got a lead and kept all job information strictly to ourselves. I soon learned that diving jobs were scarce, so I ended up with lots of time on my hands. Since Singapore was the hub of Asia, there were lots of night clubs and jazz bars to go to. I spent many nights in a variety of places and began to appreciate Asian music. Two of my friends told me I had to get my visa renewed every two weeks so we also went to resorts in Malaysia for weekends. Besides the sun, water and sand we renewed our visas whenever we came back into the country. This kept me up to date as well as busy with my social life. We had the system working well for us. The only thing I lacked was employment.

Two long months went by and I still had no work. I began to wonder if this dream would ever happen or if I would chalk this up simply to an extended vacation. I had moved to a YMCA youth hostel in the meantime, another notch or two down the ladder of hotels as finances became more and more of an issue. The "Y" cost $2/day and if you caught or killed a rat the day's rent was free. Hotel life now seemed in the distant past. The Y was a pretty basic place, with salamanders on the walls and a shared shower with a bunch of other guys.

Time went by. Two days before Christmas I was down to my last $200. I was fairly certain I'd be calling my parents for air fare in a couple of days and would soon be on a flight home. In a burst of optimism and never one to let reality stand in my way, I walked out of the hostel to place an order for Christmas flowers to be sent to my Mom. I passed a church on my walk and, desperate, went in, knelt down and prayed, "God, if you get me a job, I'll serve you for the rest of my life" having no actual knowledge or care for God at all. I figured at that point I had nothing to lose so might as well try God, though it was an empty promise made in the dry dust of desperation. Feeling rather empty and hoping none of my friends had seen me, I left the church, having had no visions or voices and walked dejectedly down Orchard Road. I came to the IGN building where the dive company Sea Tec had their offices. I had been down this road many times before. Lifting my head, I resolved to try Sea Tec one more time, and with nothing to lose I went to the fourteenth floor, a familiar office where I'd applied many times before. The manager came out of his office and asked me to come in immediately for an interview. I wasn't exactly sure why he was suddenly so interested in me. I showed him my Seneca College certificate and, to my absolute astonishment, he offered me a job on the spot. I was to start on a drill ship in the South China Sea in two weeks. I had a one-year contract and they would pay me $1,400 US a month! In those days, to a young guy hungry for work, this was a huge sum. The manager told me not to tell the other guys. When I left the building I ordered a huge bouquet for Mom, called my parents, then went back to the hostel and of course shared the secret with everyone I saw. In all the grand excitement, my promise to God faded into the background, as expected. However, I believe that though I shunted my hasty promise to the back of my memory and soon forgot, God did not.

Two weeks passed quickly and I soon found myself working on an oil rig. The rig was basically a big ship with an open hatch in the middle and from this hatch they drilled for oil. The drilling process was complicated, noisy and dangerous. We divers had to take cement samples and do maintenance on the drilling apparatus. There were five divers on each team. We only worked when needed or called so we spent a lot of boring time painting and cleaning the ship, just to stay active and deserving of our pay. The company tried to keep us busy and close by so we could be called at a moment's notice.

There were lots of water snakes, I'd see them twisting in the water. These were totally unexpected by a beginner whose training to date had been in a pool or small inland lake. When I first began my diving here, I wasn't sure how I'd react to my first encounter with one of these creatures. Surprisingly, I felt no fear of them or revulsion to them at all. There were also lots of Tiger sharks and dolphins, all basically harmless. It seemed they had adjusted to having us invading their home and environment. It never occurred to me in those days to be nervous about unexpected behavior from these creatures. Once on a dive a barracuda swam right by me. I can still see the row of sharp teeth in its mouth and recall the thud of my heartbeat.

In the beginning we trained in a bell and decompression chamber deep in the water beneath our ship. On one of our diving sessions during my training period I was supposed to put on my KB10 mask which had a spider web harness to clip to my helmet. In my haste and eagerness to get going I only did up a couple of snaps on my helmet, locked quickly out of the underwater diving bell and turned on the air. Immediately and totally unexpectedly, the force of the air blew my half-secured helmet off with a neck-wrenching blast since it wasn't snapped properly. Feeling somewhat disoriented and wondering just what had attacked me, I found myself outside of the bell and without my helmet, facing a serious situation. I had to make a quick decision that could save my life or end it – try for the surface thirty feet above me or get back to the bell. Instinctively I kicked desperately back to the safety of the nearby bell and, in seconds, clawed my way back in, my heart beating like a sledgehammer in my chest. This turned out to be the right choice. In all likelihood the air hose would have actually prevented me from reaching the surface had I gone in that direction and could have trapped me, causing me to drown immediately. My adrenaline-charged heart took its good time to quiet down to the point that I could analyze what had just happened.

When my heart resumed its normal beat, I acted as if nothing had happened, ever the cool, unflappable male. I still thought I was invincible. Nothing could bring me down. After an experience like that anyone else might have quit on the spot, but not me. I was back on the job immediately.

Apart from that near death experience, I enjoyed the water there. It was clean and beautiful, not like I was used to in the Niagara River. Even at night you could see beautiful fish in the clear ocean pool. Some of the workers would fish off the ship and we had fresh red snapper every Friday. The food was delicious. The company fed us well – steak and ice cream along with the seafood. Despite all my exercise each day, I started to put on extra weight.

Since I was making pretty good money I started sending some home regularly to pay back my loan at the bank. The balance on my loan dropped quickly and I was able to save a significant amount in a short time. It soon became apparent, however that the luster of this exciting life was beginning to wear off. Despite the glamour on the surface, Singapore seemed like a very Americanized place to me. Everyone was making money, chasing their dreams. It was all about modern progress. The city was crowded with tall skyscrapers and huge office buildings. At night they would glow brightly with the lights from people working late in thousands of offices. It bustled with the never-ending life of trade and commerce. But I soon realized I didn't really enjoy life there and it began to feel empty and achingly lonely. We worked "shifts" – two weeks on the rigs and one week off. After two days on the oil rigs I wished I was back at the youth hostel with friends, and after two days at the youth hostel, I wished I was back on the oil rig. It was quickly becoming a cycle of boredom with no end in sight. There was a lot of night life and excitement in the city in contrast with the adventure and danger on the rig. But I couldn't put my finger on the restlessness and loneliness deep in my soul. I enjoyed the time I spent there, but I guess you can say I just wasn't happy.

Looking back on my time in Asia and the years immediately following my return to Canada, I realize I was looking for something. Like all young men there was a yearning for some sort of adventure or accomplishment in my heart. Perhaps I was a bit young for the questions that swirled in my head, but I never seemed to find my niche. I could never seem to finish things. As soon as I was on one life project, I had to find the next one. I got homesick in Singapore - tired of wine, women and song, if you can believe it at age twenty-one. There were parties every night, liquor and lots of available women. Deep inside, however, with all this going on around me, there was a sense of being lost and alone. I lost touch with my buddies in Singapore soon after I returned home. Somehow their friendships were only based on our shared diving experiences and couldn't survive a normal life back in Canada.

After a year in Singapore, with my loan paid back in full, I decided to return to Fort Erie. I can't say I was disappointed to leave, but knew without doubt that that part of my life was finished. By then I had saved enough money for a down payment on a house. In short order I proudly purchased my first home, a one storey, two-bedroom bungalow on Pound Avenue. At that time it was out in the country and had a large yard with many trees. I loved that house and was proud of what I'd accomplished. It was a good starter home, my castle. I felt like an important young guy in the small town of Fort Erie. I'd already done what few would ever do in their lives and been where few would even venture to go. I had some status and was sure the next success of my life awaited me just around the corner. I was in the process of landscaping the property when I got sick and eventually had to give it up, losing everything I had invested in it.

It was 1983. I landed a full time job at Greater Canada Colour, a printing company that produces comics and newspaper advertising. I also worked as a helper for a handyman. I don't know how I got that job. I can barely hammer in a nail without destroying a complete wall! I also had a series of other odd jobs in the area.

Soon after my return to Fort Erie, I noticed how much I missed Asian culture and the people I had grown to love in the short time I had spent in Singapore. My experiences in South East Asia had become an essential part of who I was. I took several courses at Brock University in

Asian Studies and culture. Was this another sign of not knowing where I belonged, or was it another important piece of the greater puzzle of my life coming together over a long period of time?

I enrolled in a welding program at Niagara College for a year to brush up on my skills, thinking I could get better employment with this trade. After I graduated I got a job at Harbor Craft Manufacturing in Fort Erie working on robotics, a brand new field. I also did riveting on boats and welded wood burning stoves. If you have one of these stoves and the handle has fallen off, I probably welded it. If your aluminum boat leaks, I probably did the riveting. Remember, my "handiness" was limited. Thinking back on those days in that shop, it's certainly a miracle that I didn't burn off my hands or lose my eyesight.

In those years I made an effort to develop a social life. I attended a number of community events such as dances and parties on a regular basis. One night there was a dance at the Fort Erie race track. It was here that I spotted two girls with another man. One of the girls in particular caught my eye. I decided I had to meet her so I built up my nerve (maybe it was the beer!), went over to their table and asked if the two women were sisters! What a line – eh? After some conversation, I finally asked the younger girl to dance and she said yes. The next morning at 8:30 I called her and asked her to go to a movie. I wonder now if she thought I was desperate. We had a great time on that date.

CHAPTER 3
STRESS, REALITY
and FANTASY

I didn't realize it at the time but I'd entered a period of my life that would forever change me and shape my future. The aimlessness of not knowing my personal direction combined with relationships that were developing in my life would soon take me to places I would never have imagined and indeed deep into my own personal hell. At the time, of course, I had no idea. I just figured I was the luckiest guy in Fort Erie with a new girlfriend.

Her name was Cassie. I fell deeply in love with her, or so I thought. I thought I'd entered heaven and immediately became oblivious to the rest of the world. As is quite often the case with a young guy, I'm quite sure she didn't love me as much as I thought I loved her. I was infatuated with her. My mind was thinking of her every hour of the day. Of course, what I couldn't see was that we were very incompatible. For example, she was a late night person, and would sleep late every day. I was exactly the opposite. She was very artistic and seemed to see the world differently. I admired this in her and thought she was very intelligent. It seemed she had a close family while I didn't. She was punk before punk reached North America. She dyed her hair bright colours. She had looks, personality and an artistic flair. She was often impulsive and would go places and do things that would never enter my head. But I was drawn to this, since I too saw myself as adventurous in a whole different way. I knew I had lucked out in a big way and always wondered why she continued to go out with me.

After dating Cassie for a while I got to know some of her friends. One of them was a girl named Finnizia. On a whim, I invited her to stop by my house one day and to my surprise she showed up. We soon started a secret relationship, although I never really had any feelings for her. She told me she couldn't have kids. This was great for me – all the fun of a secret, with no strings relationship attached and no responsibility. But, it wasn't true as I soon learned. Finnizia did get pregnant. I was jolted into reality by this and realized my terrible carelessness. Immediately I suggested she have an abortion, hoping the "problem" would just go away. She refused and I went on with my life, trying to ignore the pregnancy and the accompanying responsibilities that were soon to come as a result of my reckless behavior. Inside I was greatly ashamed of my actions and suppressed the strong feelings of shame and guilt, refusing to discuss it or deal with it at all. My actions were a huge deal to me, causing me intense stress inside.

The complications of relationships with three people - two women and an unborn child began to take a toll on me. I was dealing with guilt, fear and embarrassment all at one time. I felt like I was being pushed from every side, inside and out and for the first time in my life, began to doubt my ability to cope with reality. I had nobody to turn to and nowhere to run. There was no place to hide from my own mistakes. Time went on but I felt a tightening pressure building inside me. I hid it on the outside and I thought nobody knew, but inside I was a mess of conflicting thoughts and emotions. Sleep became impossible and I was soon irritable and cranky with friends.

Mr. and Mrs. MacPhee;

Bill was a very responsible, above average student.

He worked at Riches and at a printing place in Stevensville. "He never wanted to do manual labour," said Bill's dad, John William MacPhee.

After high school Bill went to Seneca College and got his deep sea divers ticket and his welding ticket. He was eighteen.

As soon as he graduated from Seneca College he was off to Singapore. He lived in the slums of Singapore. There were rats and it was terrible. While living there Bill got a job on a drilling rig in the China Sea. He was making pretty good money and he would send money home to pay off his bank loan. After one year Bill returned with enough money for the down payment on a house. The house was on Pound Avenue, behind the Cottage Kitchen, a small local restaurant, and Bill lived there alone.

Bill was always a seeker. He got a job at the Press working ten hours a day. Bill fell in love with a girl named Cassie who didn't want anything to do with him. Bill then got involved with Cassie's friend and they had a child. Somehow Bill also got involved with the Jehovah's Witnesses around this time and they started instructing him in their theology. The Jehovahs were at his house on a regular basis.

At about the same time as I was dealing with all the personal stress in my life, another development occurred that would have long range effects on me.

One day I was raking leaves in my yard and, unexpectedly, a man and a woman came around the corner of my house. They started talking to me, offering me literature. I told them I wasn't interested, but they were very persistent and came back at least once a week. They were Jehovah's Witnesses. They were very friendly and seemed to genuinely care about me. They entered my life at a point in time when I already felt like I was standing on the side of a cliff, one small stumble away from destruction. I had no idea then, but it was their influence that would actually tip me over the edge of the abyss I had already approached in my life. It wasn't their religion or their message, just the intensity they generated inside me as I eventually got further into their teaching. It was like I was wound up in a tight ball of twine with a person on each side winding the string tighter and tighter.

At the time I would have called myself an atheist but surprisingly these people awoke in me a new realization about God. I read their book "Creation vs. Evolution" and became convinced there was a God. I became very sure of this in my mind. My two new friends invited me to the Kingdom Hall so I went. I became very excited and thought I'd found my answers. I studied the Bible intensely, believing I had found the forgiveness I so desperately craved. In all likelihood I was searching for peace and began to believe I had found the answers to the confusion in my life. They told me they couldn't believe how fast I picked things up. Things happened, weird supernatural things. To me at that time, these confirmed the answers I was seeking. My parents knew I was studying with the Witnesses almost from the beginning. My Dad later told me, "When you were doing this you were happier than a pig in shit."

Almost immediately my life began to revolve completely around my new-found faith. I believed the more I participated, the closer I would draw to resolution of my own intense problems. What I didn't realize was that I was simply adding more baggage on top of the massive burdens I was already carrying around with me, compounding the effects. I was not coming to any place of peace, but rather moving toward increasing conflict and confusion. I realize now I was well on my way into a delusional mental state called paranoia. Friends of mine, Dan and Kelly Hanuska, advised me to slow down and ignore the intensity of my new-found religion. They could tell something was happening to me. There were many signs that something was wrong, but I was unable to identify and recognize what was going on at that time.

For instance, one day I got in my car and drove the thirty kilometer stretch of the Queen Elizabeth Highway that joins Fort Erie to Niagara Falls seven times. As my thoughts became more and more tied to biblical events I had read, I believed I was circling Jericho like the Israelite children of long ago. They walked around that city seven times, and I was convinced I had to do the same. In this way reality and fantasy often became blurred in my life. Another time I went speeding down the QEW at a high speed. My car spun out and I crossed the highway, drove through the ditch, and ended up in a field. I still don't know how I got out of that one without a scratch on my body, it truly amazes me. At the time I believed I was being protected and prepared for a divine mission or purpose that was to come later.

I was the centre of my plan, the master plan. Everything meant something. When I saw the Minolta Tower lights flashing, it was a message to me. Print in the Bible would come off the page and widen. Knots on barn wood would expand and contract. I saw faces in the knot work. Some of them were demons that I had to expel. When I listened to the dialogue on TV shows like Seinfeld, there would be messages for me. When the camera zoomed in on someone's face on TV, I believed it was part of the master plan. I thought I could reverse time by making eye contact with someone. But it didn't work if the person was wearing glasses. But if the person took off his glasses, I took it as a message to me. It wasn't a coincidence, it was part of the master plan of getting everyone "back to reality." Coincidences backed up my delusions. I liked Olivia Newton John's music and also Neil Diamond's. I went to a friend's house and I heard them on the radio. This was a great message to me. I had no idea I was ill. I thought it was all a great religious experience. I was special - the centre of the universe - and God was communicating with me. Fire halls and nursing homes were built for me.

It seemed pressure was converging on me. I was very intense, studying all the time, reading scripture and seeing "visions." I would wake up in the night at 2AM and read because I couldn't sleep. I believed supernatural things were happening all around me. While I was reading the Bible I would watch the print float off the page, expand and widen and circle above me. I remember being scared, not knowing why all of these strange events were happening around me, but at the same time I knew this was happening to me for a reason. I thought I was being gifted with a deep understanding of cults and doctrine. My psychosis and delusions had started, and everything that I did or saw was magnified and intensified to the extreme. In fact my life was getting out of control, about to explode and I had no way of stopping it. I was entering a stage of acute psychosis. Crucial lines between reality and fantasy were very blurred and I was increasingly unable to tell the difference between them.

I was taught by my Jehovah's Witness friends to have no contact with my parents, so that anchor and support system gradually became absent from my life. My friends had decided that I was too hard to hang out with since I seemed to live in a different world than theirs. The life I was living was overwhelming and exhausting, but I was in too deep to be able to turn back. The Jehovah's Witnesses had a central belief in which they were looking for the chosen one to come. In my mind and with my complete focus on myself, I became the fulfillment of that belief. The universe and all its purposes were to be found in me, Bill MacPhee. I was the chosen one and with this new position, it was my responsibility to bring the whole world back to its original state of paradise. I had been given a huge responsibility along with a position of authority and power. It would be like the Garden of Eden and I would be the new

Adam and my girlfriend Cassie would be the new Eve. I thought the universe, the cosmos and time all had to go backwards to this original state. In my mind by way of a huge time warp I was the new Christ who would fix all the ills of the world, particularly matching up the right people so all would be happy and compatible. Cassie and I would tease people, and by teasing them we would bring them together. This was for "genetic purification." Cassie and I would be on earth for 1,000 years and we would never get old. The fate of the entire cosmos rested on my shoulders. I had been specially chosen to fulfill the destiny of all mankind. I believed all of this.

I don't recall if I ever advised Cassie about her great role in the revamping of the whole universe. She might have wondered about my sanity, with good reason.

Sometime in this short period I vaguely wondered if I was becoming "mentally ill." However my knowledge of this type of illness was extremely limited. Any questioning was momentary at best. Instead I thought I was having deeply religious experiences. Of course this interpretation further enhanced the intensity of my thoughts. The line between reality and fantasy was becoming increasingly blurred. I didn't know what to think. There were times I believed God was communicating to me alone and that I was the extreme centre of the universe. What I didn't realize at the time was that I was about to enter the most agonizing, confused period of my life. You might call this the "lost years." I was seriously ill and my very life was in danger from my own mental journey. The next five years would involve a roller coaster ride of huge highs and deep lows as my illness took hold. It is truly a miracle that I'm alive today. I was far closer to actual death than I ever knew. All of this took place deep within my own brain and I shared it with nobody. The more bizarre my thinking became, the more I was certain I had to keep it a close secret.

CHAPTER 4

SECRETS and CRISIS – "Beam Me Up Scotty"

My belief that I was having deeply religious experiences, that I was special and God was communicating with me alone kept me from seeing any part of the real world. So I had no idea I was desperately ill and getting sicker with every passing day. With each new "revelation," it became more apparent that I was the centre of the universe, I had special powers and it was my job to make the world a better place. My mission was clear: I had been chosen above the millions of other people to save the world. It was no small task, but I was more than willing to embark on this great feat. I became convinced I could reverse time back to a better world, I was the new Adam. This image was gradually becoming the centre of my life. Words, lights and the smallest coincidences each held great meaning for me as I became the chosen one. Gradually, over a period of time, my world drew inward as this vision took complete control of my existence.

Everywhere I turned I thought I was being given special messages and signals. Through television shows, newspapers, radio, there were secret codes everywhere that were known only to me. . For example the word "original" became a key word because as I saw it, it was my job to get the world back to its "original" state. Original New York Seltzer held a special meaning. I was drawn to the shiny labels on the bottles. I drank cases of this seltzer and basically stopped eating. As a result my physical health deteriorated along with my mental condition. When I was shopping I had trouble deciding what to buy. Oranges – Israel, Jafa, and Sunkist – all of the names meant something to me. I believed I could magically unlock doors. In psychosis there's a "magic." Every small detail of life was crucial, magical. If I read the word "witness" in the newspaper, it was a secret message to me. If someone said "O God," I believed I was being called because I was God. I remember one night mentioning the beatitudes to my Dad. He opened a Bible right to the passage. I truly believed I controlled that. I often heard the song by Billy Vera and the Beaters "What did you think I would do at this moment?" I thought this was God asking me, talking to me through the song. The night I drove to Niagara Falls seven times, the lights on the highway were codes. I thought I had to destroy molecules, like the micro organisms in plasma and water. The radiator in my car overheated, and it meant something.

At the same time I was carrying a huge load of personal stress, building daily toward a sharp point of crisis. In the real world I had been "raised right," yet here I had a child out of wedlock. Others, including my parents thought I was nice, but deep down inside I was ashamed. They couldn't see the real me. I kept my real self carefully hidden. I couldn't forget my past. I was convinced more and more that I would be found out and there would be consequences for my sin. I lived daily with the awful fear that somehow others could see through the thin veneer of respectability I so desperately painted on each day. I often felt sure someone would discover my fraudulent self and reveal it to the whole world. Maybe God would write it on my forehead if I didn't confess. I had great expectations for my future that I thought I would never be able to accomplish; it felt like my life was over. I would never be able to achieve the successes of my father and wouldn't have money for my son as my father had for me during my young years. My brother Tom's wife was beautiful, Finn wasn't. All these thoughts constantly swirled inside my head, like a windstorm or a tornado with no outlet.

I believed I had to get the world back to its original state – paradise - with lots of food, happiness and everyone getting along. It would be like the Garden of Eden before sin. I would be the new Adam and Cassie would be the new Eve. I thought time had to go backward so the world could get to its original state. This would happen by time travel, back to the time when Christ was with God in heaven. I believed Christ had come back in another generation, so time had to reverse for Christ to come back. I thought the universe, the cosmos and time all had to go backwards. In my world this was accomplished by me turning around backwards and looking in the mirror.

Another part of my thinking was that I had to get the right people matched up, all the way back to the beginning of time. At one point, on a high, I thought Cassie and I would have a fun time on earth. We would tease people and by doing so would bring them together. They would laugh and relax. We had to do this because people were meant to be together. We were to do this for "genetic purification." Cassie and I would be on the earth for 1,000 years and we'd never get old.

One night in February of 1987 I was at home and the thought came to me that I had to go to meet Cassie. It was a clear night, one of the coldest of the year. I was suddenly convinced this was it. The time had come for me to fulfill my purpose, what I was sent here to do. I had to go and find Cassie, and then we would meet people and match them up together to create a new paradise. It was all coming to completion according to the pre-arranged plan. I was the new Adam, Cassie the new Eve. After a long shower during which I became very confused I dressed and drove down Garrison Road, the main highway in Fort Erie. After a few kilometers I stopped the car and got out to walk, leaving my vehicle running and unlocked. It was freezing cold outside. The thought came to me that I had to prove myself worthy to God. Like Abraham, I had to prove my faith. So I walked on the highway, in the traffic, cars veering around me from both directions. To me the headlights were attractive colors refracting all around me.

I should be clear at this point – this was not a suicide attempt. There was no thought of taking my life in this event. I was very aware of the mission I was on and nothing could stop me. Every detail was intricately clear to me. The path before me had been determined by the Almighty and I was following His decree.

As I was walking down the highway I clearly recall seeing a sign that the great final battle of all time, Armageddon was about to occur. A jet flew overhead with a loud, deafening noise. It seemed to me I was walking down a long tunnel. There was a light at the end of the tunnel. I started walking around a bend in the tunnel, around the corner of the road. Something big was going to happen! This was the beginning of my mission.

Thirsty, I walked across the street to a convenience store, picked up a chocolate milk and a bag of chips, and walked out without paying. The clerk did nothing, perhaps afraid of me. I wonder what he saw and thought as I walked through his store that dark night. Was he part of the plan? Did he call the police? Many years later, after my recovery, I went back into this store and paid for the items.

I continued my trek down the highway, on my mission to prove myself worthy to God. I was wondering how it would all work out when the amazing and yet meaningless thought crossed my mind that I didn't need anything. If I had God, there was nothing else in this world that I needed, not even the clothes on my back. Piece by piece I undressed, walking zombie-like through speeding traffic. There I was, naked on a highway in the middle of winter. Piercing February temperatures of minus 10 Celcius met my skin, but I didn't feel any pain, discomfort or humiliation. This was what I was meant to do, what God wanted me to do. I was standing naked near a streetlight and bizarrely recall thinking, "Beam me up Scotty" like on Star Trek. In my mind I was the prophet, the Christ, the chosen one. It was extremely real for me. I was not ill. The Roman guards soon arrived, sent to arrest and slaughter the Christ.

In reality the police came to save me from walking any further down the middle of the highway to certain injury or death, not to mention frostbite. In my mind I knew they were looking for the new Messiah and they would know I was the chosen one. I knew I would be resurrected so Cassie and I could be together to make the new world. I was full of fear and horror, but also very sure of my purpose. This was all part of the master plan for me. I wonder what the police officers thought when they came across a naked fat guy in the middle of the highway on a cold February night? In hindsight, the officers' actions reflected a certain balance of stern authority and kind humanity toward a very sick individual. I remember those streetlights in particular, they were fascinating. I thought the world would get back to its original state through light. After all, God is light! Living by the Niagara River, I knew there was cleansing power in the lights. Everything flowed in the river, so in my mind the lights on Niagara Falls purified everything that went over the falls at the molecular level.

I'm not sure how they managed to do it, but after the officers got me in the back seat of the cruiser and wrapped me in a blanket I was first taken to our local hospital in Fort Erie. I was examined quickly by a doctor and almost immediately sent on to the hospital in Niagara Falls to properly diagnose and treat my situation.

In the ambulance on the way to Niagara Falls I couldn't tell anybody what was really happening. To them there was something wrong. I was ill, in trouble, and needed help, but I was well aware of what was going on. I was carrying a great secret of the universe, and I had to keep it inside because nobody would believe me. I was fearful and the voices told me not to tell. If others found out, my mission would be jeopardized. When I was admitted, the doctors began asking me questions about my condition and what had happened that night. I gave vague, muddled answers designed to prevent them from discovering the truth that only I could understand. I was purposely uncooperative and uncommunicative, because I couldn't yet reveal the universal secret that was being played out. The next part of the mission would be my death on a cross. **"BILL MACPHEE HAS TO DIE,"** then be resurrected, I thought. I learned later this is classic behavior for mentally ill people. The room I was placed in had a plaque on the wall that recognized a family that had made a donation to the hospital. Once again I saw this as a sign. I thought I would die and be resurrected as the new prophet, like Jesus and my new name was being given to me through this plaque on the wall. It was all part of the wonderful plan. "They" would fake my death and I would come forth resurrected as this person with the new name. All the arrangements had been made for me. It was all being worked out according to the master plan.

Mr. MacPhee:

> *On the night it happened, Bill decided he was going to go to church. On his way there he decided to get out of his car and walk down the highway. He thought he was Jesus Christ and he stripped down. The police came and took him to the hospital. Jeff Douglas came to get me at the school where I was playing bridge and told me what had happened to my son. Bill stayed in the hospital all night and saw Dr. Mitchell. What happened that night came as a shock to all of us. There had been no signs of an impending breakdown. Bill was so with it, we never could have imagined that happening.*

Feb. 4-12, 1987 – Dr. Mitchell

- *Bill picked up naked, shouting religious slogans, by police who took him to the hospital in Ft. Erie where he was seen by Dr. Lee.*
- *Transferred to emergency, examined by Dr. Chakreburtty: found to be agitated, uncommunicative, exhibiting peculiar gestures.*

Examined by Dr. Mitchell: refused to talk, appeared Bill had become acutely psychotic. Given Haldol, Cogentin and Halcion.

- *Two days later Bill left hospital in gown, no shoes – was found in Public Health Building. Staff thought he might be hallucinating.*
- *Bill was discharged – to return for follow-up in two weeks, continued Haldol at bedtime.*

Feb. 4, 1987 Hospital Consultation Record

This 24 year old man was transferred from the hospital in Fort Erie after he was brought to the Emergency Room by the police. He apparently had been found outside, in the nude, talking irrationally and shouting religious slogans. According to Dr. M. Lee, who examined him at the hospital, he has no previous history of psychiatric illness, although he has an older brother who apparently has been treated on a number of occasions for psychiatric illness. According to Dr. Lee, his mother reports that this man has been preoccupied with religion for the past several weeks, and has been spending a good deal of time reading the bible and other religious material. Dr. Lee put this man on a Form 1 and he was sent to our Emergency Room. He was examined by Dr. Chakreburtty, who found him to be agitated, uncommunicative, and exhibiting peculiar gestures.

On my examination, Mr. MacPhee refuses to talk. He closes his eyes during most of the examination. Occasionally he will make a blowing motion with his lips. It is not possible to sample his thought processes in view of his refusal to speak.

It would appear from the observations of others and his present mental state that he has become acutely psychotic. He is being admitted for a period of assessment and treatment.

Feb. 4, 1987 – Nurses notes

2250 – Services: Dr. Mitchell. Diagnosis: Acute psychotic state. Patient. placed in limb restraints, segufix, not communicating to staff, Sitting up in bed, blowing, in attempt to make staff disappear. Found running outside without clothes on. Pt. remained in four limb restraints, segufix.

SEGUFIX

A universal system of securing patients in psychiatric departments. It is designed to be affixed to a hospital bed. It includes fixative belts for arms, shoulders, chest, abdomen, thighs, ankles and a wide belt for fixing the patient to the bed.

Feb 5, 1987 – Nurses Notes

2300—0700 – received in segufix, 4 limb restraints, appears to be sleeping. Awoke at 0215, appears to be hallucinating, talking to self, curved over in bed, guarded, restraints too tight. Adjustments made and attempts to make patient comfortable. Refusing medication. Uncooperative, quiet. Sleeping long periods. 2 ½ hour surveillance. Dr. Mitchell in at 0815. Right hand taken out of restraint for breakfast, ate well. Remaining 3 restraints taken off at 0930. He insists when asked that last night's behavior wasn't characteristic of him. Says he'll be cooperative, is agreeable to staying in hospital. Parents shocked Bill struck an orderly. 1500 – Remains only in segufix abdominal restraint. A restful day. 1500-2300 – Received in segufix, asleep. Slept until 1700 when awakened for supper. Stated he was hot, hungry, but refused dinner, drank two cups of juice. Visited briefly with patient, who was sleeping lightly but aware of our presence. Parents wondering what to expect as patient has never been mentally ill before.

As described in the doctor's notes, I was picked up by the police walking naked in the middle of the highway shouting religious slogans and was quickly taken to the hospital. After a quick examination by Doctor Lee, I was transported to the emergency at Niagara Hospital. My actions were described as agitated, uncommunicative and exhibiting peculiar gestures. I remember as I was wheeled down the hallway of the hospital I was desperately planning my escape, trying to figure out how I could get out. At the end of the hall was a big, muscular orderly, the only thing standing in the way of me and my freedom. All around, arrows were pointing me in the right direction, the path of escape, but that path was being blocked by that evil orderly. Voices were telling me I had to get out, and I knew what I had to do. I eyed him up, and he looked back at me. He was tall, muscular and dressed all in white. He looked evil, and I didn't like him. In all likelihood he was simply an ordinary guy doing his job completely unaware of my psychotic anger about to explode on him. When we were close enough to him, I sprang up from the cold wheelchair and attacked him, punching him in the face and knocking out one of his teeth. Blood gushed from his face, staining his crisp white uniform. Immediately I was given a shot to knock me out and put into a hospital restraint device, called segufix. It was a type of straitjacket, that could be fastened to a hospital bed. They gave me a cocktail of drugs – Haldol, Cogentin and Halcion. When I came to, I had no idea how long I had been out, but I remember being groggy and drowsy. I was still having hallucinations and knew I needed to get out. Two days later I left the hospital in a gown with no shoes. They found me in the Public Health Building nearby. Staff thought I was hallucinating. Other reports on my behavior during these first weeks include my refusal to communicate with staff and I often sat up and blew with my mouth. In my mind this would make them disappear! During this period, at times my behavior was seemingly normal, and at other times I was hostile or uncommunicative and had to be in restraints. I slept for lengthy periods of time, perhaps because of sedation.

CHAPTER 5
HOSPITAL

My parents came to visit me nearly every day. I wish to acknowledge their efforts and thank them for their simple, loving support. They were devoted to me. Mom would bring me food – mostly apples and bananas. We discussed things briefly but mostly they would just sit with me. Sometimes we went to the TV room or played ping pong. We didn't talk a lot, but it wasn't the words we shared or the length of the conversations that I valued. They were there for me when I was at the lowest point in my life, and that is something that I will never forget and will always be thankful for. But even while they were with me, in my delusional state I often paced, back and forth, back and forth.

I always took my medication, which would leave me zombie-like and groggy. Everything seemed to happen so fast around me, but I felt like I was moving in slow motion and unable to keep up. At first, even while on medication I continued to think all my delusions were true but nobody else "got it." So, to keep my secrets, I had to pretend I was normal and all was okay. I would straighten up and fake it so they wouldn't figure out my secrets. The plan was still in place to be carried out. I was always on the lookout for things that went along with the plan, including people who might have special knowledge that I needed. I saw myself as some new kind of infant, that I was obtaining great power. But I didn't know how to use it. It was too dangerous for me to have all the power at once so I had to get the information from other people a little at a time. An example of this was Dave Kendrick, a local church member and a strong Christian, who studied the Jehovah's Witness beliefs. The first time I met Dave I asked him if he knew anything about theology. He said he knew a little. I asked him if he believed the grasshoppers in the bible were armored helicopters. Dave replied some people believed that.

You see, the Master Plan was still unfolding. There was God the Father, God the Son and God the Holy Spirit. Dan, my church mentor, was the Father, and I thought I was the Son (I didn't know who was the Spirit). In my mind this was a check and balance situation. I thought that as the new Christ I had all kinds of power, but I was balanced by Dan so I wouldn't go corrupt. People above me knew my plan, they would harness my power and guide me. I was so happy when my new friend Dave Kendrick started his visits. I initially believed he was sent to lead me to the next steps and guide me through the months and events that lay ahead. It was all still going according to the Master Plan.

I couldn't understand why Dan, my former teacher, and his wife didn't come to visit me though. Dan was the one who had lead me to great truths in my new faith. I tried to get to a phone to call them. I learned later that my brother Tom had called them, threatened them and told them emphatically to stay away from me.

I slowly began to realize I was in a mess. At times I felt and acted "normal" while at other times my delusions took over my whole being. In my psychotic periods the magical powers still remained. It was "enjoyable" to a degree. I held the magic and the power! But when a sense of normality would return I began to realize I was in a mess.

During this period, unknown to me, my mother's sister, Gert Sherk, who attended the Sherkston Brethren In Christ church had informed my Mom a person in the church named Dave Kendrick had a special ministry to Jehovah's Witness believers. My Dad contacted Dave and asked him to see me. He said he would but he wasn't sure what he could do because he didn't know much about mental illness. Dave first came to meet me in the hospital. I was lying in bed heavily sedated. They tell me when I woke up we immediately began discussing theology. I remember him sitting in the chair beside my bed. He asked me if I believed the Bible. I asked him about the helicopters and Armageddon. I remember feeling very happy – Dave would tell me. He would lead me to the next step. I trusted him. I asked Dave about the torture stake. The Jehovah's Witnesses believe Jesus died on this instead of the cross. I also mentioned to Dave the "H" on the hospital sign was turning into a swastika.

Dave came back to see me frequently. He was concerned for me and treated me as a person. Dave became a close friend. He spent a lot of his free time with me. When I was first released from the hospital I was often at Dave's house having tea and sharing a meal. I recall that summer I went to my Dad's cottage with Dave and his family. I had nightmares and Dave would bring me water. Dave was quiet and gentle, he liked to talk to people.

Cassie also came to visit me one time while I was in the hospital. I was in the recreation room when she walked in. We had a brief conversation. Later one of the attendants told me, "You must have liked her, you really brightened when you saw her." I tried to tell her I wasn't sick or crazy, that something supernatural was going on. I believed I was normal and tried to convince her my thoughts were true.

My first medication was Haldol. It was an anti-psychotic drug. I constantly paced up and down the hallway of the hospital and always felt like I needed to urinate, but couldn't go. I didn't hang around with anybody else. I watched a lot of TV – Magnum PI at 4pm was my favorite.

I was still delusional. I would sit for long periods and stare out the window at the sun. It's a miracle my eyes weren't fried and I can see at all today. I was like a zombie. When they first let me go outside for brief periods, the cars all appeared to be speeding by at impossible speeds. They were travelling way too fast. I thought I would never drive again. In group therapy I was slow to respond to anything. My actions had slowed to the point of barely moving. I felt like I was underwater all the time, trying to push a huge wave of water wherever I went.

Feb. 6, 1987 Progress Note, Dr. Mitchell

This young man is quite alert now. Initially he was somewhat sedated on the Haldol but I have reduced the dosage. Yesterday he seemed more rational however despite his somnolence from the Haldol. He was able to give a rational account of his background. He recalled taking his clothes off but could give no reason why he did this. I gathered from what he said that he had been preoccupied with religion since August or September 1986. He had given up playing racquetball, had become withdrawn from friends and spent most of his free time reading religious literature.

According to the nursing staff the patient has been less well today. He has made some rather peculiar but vague phrases indicating to the nursing staff that he might be experiencing hallucinations. Earlier this afternoon he left the hospital clad only in a hospital gown and without foot wear after insisting that he wanted to leave hospital. He was found in the Public Health Building and returned to the Psychiatric Unit.

When I spoke to Bill tonight he initially was pleasant and responded to my greeting appropriately. He then got up and went into the bathroom and began to look in

*the mirror, talking to himself in a manner that I could
not understand and making grimaces with his mouth.
After several minutes he returned to talk with me. When
asked about his departure without appropriate clothing
he seemed unconcerned and refused to talk about it. He
requested that he be discharged. He said that no matter
what I said he was going to leave the hospital. It was
explained to him that the police would be called to return
him to the hospital and he replied, "If that is the way it is
to be so be it." Throughout most of the interview he was
making peculiar motions with his mouth and tongue. At
first I thought these had arisen from the Haldol giving rise
to a dystonic reaction, however just an hour before he had
received some Cogentin.*

*There is no doubt that this man has had a psychotic break.
He seems to have little insight into his illness and in fact I
am under the impression he is still having serious problems
relating to reality.*

In the last week of February, 1987, I was discharged from the psychiatric
unit of the Niagara hospital. I was to return for follow-up in two
weeks and continue taking Haldol at bedtime. I spent a lot of time
at Dave's house. Dave often raved about his wife Glennis' pizza. One
night I was supposed to go to their house for pizza, but instead I went
to Station B of the post office where Dave worked. I was very anxious
and felt something special would happen that night. I couldn't wait
any longer so had to see Dave. I was in a state of psychosis and began
doing jumping jacks in the small lobby of the office. The police and
ambulance were called and when they arrived I started staring intently
into the ears of one of the officers. When the officer asked me what I
was doing I replied, "Just looking." The sad humour of this is not lost
on me today, but the officer handled the situation with great calm and
understanding. Perhaps they'd heard of me before. I believed I had

special powers and could see into people's heads by looking in their ears. When the police asked me if I wanted to go to the hospital I responded, "No, I don't want to go to the hospital." At that point Dave contacted my parents and my dad came down to the post office. I trusted Dave deeply. In my mind he was "King David." Dave had a mole on the back of his right hand. I believed it looked like a scar where a nail had been driven in during a crucifixion. When Dave gently asked me if I wanted to go to the hospital, I quoted the bible saying, "No. My no means no." However, a few minutes later I was finally convinced to go to the hospital because of my trust in "King David." I recall asking Dave if I should sign the admittance papers. Dave replied yes so I signed them without further question.

Feb. 24, 1987 - Dr. Mitchell

- *Bill picked up by police for making inappropriate comments and doing calisthenics in lobby of Fort Erie post office, taken to hospital, examined by Dr. Munkly and Dr. Mitchell: found to be uncooperative and uncommunicative.*
- *Bill's father said Bill had been deteriorating for the last week.*
- *Bill admitted, Haldol increased.*

Feb 25, 1987 Clinical Record

- *23-0700 – Woke at 0345, given medicine to help resettle, no effect. Asking for towels, toothbrush and to be allowed out. Banging on door became louder and glared angrily at staff through window. Banging continues and became violent kicking by 0720 after talking with nurse through the door. After receiving medicine door was unlocked. Pt tried to bargain with nurse to stay out of his room and pushed his way out when bargaining failed. 0800 orderlies put Patient back into room and into segufix. Patient has voiced that*

*he wants his "freedom" and that it was "such a nice day outside."
After escaping from his segufix the Patient was found wandering
the hall and refused to go back to his room. After sitting on the floor
patient was pushed back into room by 3 nurses. Patient became
angry again and pushed his way out of room making threatening
motions towards nurse. Police were called and they placed patient
in segufix and 4 limb restraints. Became more cooperative after put
in restraints. 1 arm and 1 leg restraint removed. At 1515 patient
began throwing fruit at his door and using profanities when alone
but polite with staff. Removed clothes, masturbated and spat water
at staff. Keeps calling out for female co-patient. Cleaned and dressed
by male staff. Slept in 1 arm and leg restraint and segufix.*

Dave Kendrick

*During his time in the hospital Bill plugged the toilet with towels, ripped
the toilet out and ripped sections of drywall off the wall of his room. Despite
these incidents, however, I never had any fear Bill would hurt me or anyone
else. It upset me to see Bill in restraints. The anger in Bill was something
I've never seen before or since.*

Feb. 26, 1987 – nurses notes

- *Still very disturbed, shouts and yells irrationally, makes menacing
  comments, threatening gestures towards nursing staff. Social
  behavior – inappropriate. Eg. openly masturbating before staff.
  Seemingly in poor contact with reality. Has no insight into illness.
  Indicates he wants to leave hospital, but is so psychotic he couldn't
  care for himself, poses danger for others. Therefore admitted as
  involuntary patient.*

Dave Kendrick

At times Bill had a distant stare. He would look through you instead of at you. You could also tell that Bill was having a bad day by his appearance – he usually wouldn't comb his hair. When Bill was in psychosis he was beyond logic. He would say things that weren't reasonable. For example Bill and I went to lunch at Keystone Kelly's. At this time Bill was always looking for people with "special knowledge." During lunch Bill noticed a glaze on the window which made it appear there was snow on the ground in the middle of summer. Bill insisted there was snow on the ground despite my telling him it was the sun's glare on the window.

On one occasion when I came to visit Bill I brought banana-flavored candy canes. Bill had never seen these before and he thought I was magical because I had them. Bill made some very gradual progress during these days.

March 1, 1987 – nurses notes

- *Bill much better, alert, pleasant, rational. Having difficulty concentrating, but grip on reality is much improved.*

March 2, 1987 – Clinical Record

- *2300 – 0245 Woke and softly knocked on door saying he "feels better" and looks forward to getting his clothes back. Given medicine to resettle. Co-operative with appropriate behavior. Showing no religious overtones in conversation. Says he's "going to leave his religion alone for a while." Out on grounds privileges after supper and returned on time. Said he feels sad tonight. Feels like crying but he is unable to. Parents visited later that night. 2200 woke up. Appeared frightened. Had piercing preoccupied stare. Walked halls for a few minutes and resettled on own.*

March 3, 1987 – nurses notes

- *Much improved, Bill pleasant/rational but saying he's having trouble organizing thoughts.*

March 6, 1987 – nurses notes

- *Improvement maintained. Complained of muscle spasms – likely due to Loxapine – now decreased. Pleasant, cooperative. He's well enough to go home on weekend leave of absence.*

March 20, 1987 – Dr. Mitchell

- *Bill discharged*

March 23, 1987 – Angela Doherty

- *Referral by Dr. Mitchell for Bill to see Angela Doherty, Coordinator of Psychiatrist day care program at hospital.*
- *Started program March 19. Discharged from in-patient service march 20.*
- *Discussed why brought in. Said main stress in life was becoming a father. Will support child.*
- *Bill will attend day care until Dr. Mitchell says he is ready to leave.*
- *Bill's mother is manic depressive.*
- *Bill has respect for his parents, but claims little love for them.*
- *Did well in school but felt socially inadequate. Never felt satisfied with anything he did.*
- *No delusions or hallucinations.*

March 31, 1987 - Angela Doherty

- *Made daily schedule to follow.*
- *Visits girlfriend and son, William, on daily basis.*

April 7, 1987 – Angela Doherty

- *Has moved back into his own house.*

April 21-30, 1987 – Dr. Mitchell

- *Bill feeling well, wants to go to work, asking questions re: illness.*
- *Bill leaves work early, bored, frustrated, wants to go to school.*
- *Dr. Mitchell says he'll start him back on sick benefits.*

When I was in the psych ward the second time they started me on another drug, Loxapine. Immediately, my delusions and paranoia went away. They were all gone and I came back to reality. I should have been able to simply pick up where I left off and continue my life. But I knew I needed to understand what had happened to me so I read a pamphlet about my symptoms. I knew what I had – schizophrenia. This was entirely different from having a bad case of the flu or even recovering from a bad injury. Dave told me people lived with this disease and I could too but I didn't believe him. I knew my life was over. I constantly had dry mouth, I paced and had frequent convulsions – all side effects of the new drug. This medication controlled my symptoms and I was back to reality, but it was a different "reality." I learned a new term – I was insane – sick, with no job, no friends, no finances, no house. Reality was not good. I looked again at my older brother with his endless difficulties and my mother's long histories of hospitals and futile treatments. I was just like them! I knew my life was over.

CHAPTER 6

DESPAIR, DISABILITY and DELUSIONS

May 29, 1987 – Dr. Mitchell

- *Bill complains of boredom, excessive sleeping and depression, wants a reduction in Loxapine and to return to work. Dr. Mitchell wonders if Bill has bipolar type of mood disorder, or a reactive type of depression following psychotic episodes.*

May 31, 1987 – Dr. Mitchell

- *Bill readmitted to hospital, parents concerned about his depression. Dr. Mitchell wonders if Loxapine played role in genesis of depression, and if behavior on previous admissions was atypical manic.*

June 3, 1987 – Dr. Mitchell

- *Bill discharged. Dr. Mitchell's previous diagnosis of schizophreniform psychosis changes to schizoaffective disorder, in light of presentation on this admission and in view of family history.*
- *Advised to continue Parnate and Loxapine, arrangements made for day care programme.*

During the spring to fall of 1987 I was hospitalized six times. I lived with my parents. I often went by bus to Niagara Falls to visit my son William.

July 28, 1987 – Dr. Mitchell

- *Bill off all psychotic medicines for about six weeks, Feeling well, wanting to return to work.*

Oct 15, 1987 – Dr. Mitchell

- *Bill discharged from day care programme – completed to client and team satisfaction.*

As I look back at this period from the vantage point of the present, I realize there were several forces working together within me simultaneously. I was deep in the depths of despair about the value and direction of my life while I also carried my usual itch to get moving and some measure of resolve to try and never give up on life. Perhaps this personality trait deep in my being was what drove me to take small steps to forge some sort of a life for myself. Lurking in the background was my illness, always threatening the delicate balance of whatever sanity I possessed.

I knew I needed to do something, like get a job. I tried Canada Colour again. They hired me back but time went by so slowly while I worked there. I was acutely aware of my surroundings at all times with a heightened sense of anxiety. I felt people were watching me, joking about me behind my back. I felt like an outsider who didn't belong there. I believed nobody liked me. I was an empty shell and didn't stay there long. I went on disability and sick leave. But again, I couldn't just sit still. I put out some resumes and got a few printing jobs, and at the same time began taking a real estate course, thinking I might sell houses. One day, out of the blue, I got a call from a printing company in Woodstock, Ontario of all places. I had submitted my resume when I saw their name in a newspaper. I went for the interview and got the job.

I was very happy and believed God was looking after me once again. After many talks with Dave Kendrick I began to realize God was interested in me personally. I had asked Him for help and He responded. I knew I had to thank Him. Just before this time I had been at my parents' house painting for them. I was watching the 700 Club and people were calling in to tell their wonderful experiences as God answered their prayers and blessed them. I remember I got very angry, looked up at the ceiling and with my fist in the air spat out "Do something for me! Help me! You helped many others." That's when I got the interview and the job in Woodstock. I believed God helped me. Today I'm not so sure of the theology of this short conversation with God but at the time it seemed like the right conclusion. Looking back, in all likelihood I was just good at job interviews. I just couldn't keep a job once I got it! Maybe that's why I've got my own business today.

When I arrived in Woodstock I walked into a real estate building. A man came out from an office and I explained I was new to town and needed a room. He took me to lunch and said he knew some people whose mother had a room to rent. Her name was Maybelle. She was a wonderful older lady. I rented a room from her and, thinking I was now cured, all was well and I was on my way again, I went off my medication, the natural thing to do of course. I wanted to know if the illness was a fluke, hoping to persuade myself I was fine. Of course I also wanted to be rid of the annoying side effects of the medication. I found a church to attend, the pastor was a former pilot, a good man. All was going well, except that I wasn't a very good printer/pressman. I soon left that job and got another one in Guelph as a pressman in a printing shop. Every day I drove from Woodstock to Guelph and back. I immediately got very busy, attending church services almost every night or watching

TV with Maybelle. She said I should go to parties and enjoy myself but I was serious about church and witnessing to others about my faith.

Little did I realize I was repeating old patterns of flurried activity and stress that had brought havoc and destruction to my life. Gradually, the pace of my life once again ramped up to a point of no return. I was my own worst enemy.

My focus became the work of my new church so I quit the job in Guelph, with the intent of enrolling at London Bible Baptist College. I told the people at the church my plan was to do church work and witness full time. I studied my Bible six hours a day, meticulously looking up references to each verse as I read.

The symptoms of my disorder slowly began to reappear. When I listened to my stereo, lights would refract in the unit. One night in my room I stared for hours at a light bulb in a lamp when suddenly, with a pop, the lamp burned out. Naturally I saw this as a sign. My bed had bedposts attached and as a weird sort of test of faith, I tried to put out my eye by pressing it firmly on one of the posts and grinding it into my skull – but there was absolutely no damage to my eye. It was another miracle in my mind. I stared at the bright lights in the kitchen but my vision was never harmed. In my psychotic mind I was going places, I was on a mission. My delusions had returned.

This culminated one night when I began yelling in Maybelle's house. I turned furniture over, badly scaring the dear old lady. I spat on her TV and ripped pages from my bible in front of her. I went out into the street, stopped cars and literally walked up and over some of the vehicles. I walked to the Jehovah's Witness building and banged on the doors. I remember going into a convenience store and picking up some chocolate milk and chips. When the clerk rang up my purchase (no stealing this time), the total was the exact amount I had in my pockets. I wondered how this could be and concluded this meant I was special and God must be directing my path once again. My delusions of being a chosen person had returned.

Of course my antics had not gone unnoticed and soon the police showed up! They were very nice and I simply said, "I want to go home." They seemed to have some understanding of what was going on with me so instead of taking me to the local lock up, they took me to the Woodstock hospital. The next day I was transferred back to hospital in Niagara Falls. I was started on different injected medication immediately. I was right back where I'd been ten months before.

Maybelle called my parents to let them know what was going on. My friend, Roy Willick kindly went over to her place, cleaned up my mess (lots of torn bible pages) and drove my car back to Fort Erie. I was immediately put on a new medication, Fluanxol. When this began to work I once again returned to reality and moved back in with my parents when I was discharged from the hospital.

Dec. 13, 1987 – Dr. Mitchell

- *Bill couldn't find a job in Fort Erie, moved to Woodstock three months ago. He was feeling well, stopped medications.*
- *Three weeks before Dec. 13 hospital admission, Bill felt job, church and bible studies were too much – quit job, called parents.*
- *Bill brought into emergency at hospital, had torn up bible, knocking and kicking to get in church, undressed and praying on knees(???). His parents were called by landlady, police brought him in.*
- *Bill's son 9 months old by this time and lives with the baby's mother.*
- *Diagnosis schizophrenia – paranoid type, recurrence secondary to stopping maintenance treatment of Loxapine. Haldol ordered.*

Dec. 14, 1987 – Dr. Mitchell

- *Bill transferred to Niagara, admitting diagnosis: psychosis – unspecified type. Medicine switched from Haldol to Loxapine due to extrapyramidal side effects. Dr. Mitchell decides best for Bill to be on injections of antipsychotic medicines.*
- *Recommended he continue Fluaxonal and Cogentin, return for follow-up as out-patient.*

Jan. 5, 1988 – Dr. Mitchell

- *Report says Bill doing fine*

CHAPTER 7
DARKNESS AND DEPRESSION

By late December of 1987, the meds I was being given had started to work and the delusions began to disappear. Around the beginning of 1988, the delusions had all but gone and my schizophrenia symptoms were no longer controlling my life. To some extent I had taken control of my illness, but I was nowhere near recovered. Indeed the word "recovery" only came to be used much later in my journey. In the long course of this type of illness, there is no sense of direction, beginning, ending or conclusion. It's just a day-to-day grind, with each moment, each medication, each setback or achievement forming a pattern only visible from the vantage point of the future. To speak of "recovery" is to refer to a process I never thought of during those awful months. Today, I see recovery as not wanting to be anyone other than who you are at that moment. But during those long, lifeless days, I would have given anything to be somebody else.

Over the course of this year my son William was born while I was in the hospital. He was downstairs in obstetrics while I was upstairs in the psych ward. I told Dave I had never revealed to my parents the details of Finn and her pregnancy. In his wisdom, Dave promptly relayed this to them. I was guilt-ridden. One day Dave and I went down to the nursery to see William. After that I went every day to see him and hold him but there was no joy in this. Later after I was out of the hospital I took the bus to Niagara Falls weekly to see Finn and William. She lived at her father's house at the time. I was very ill and would just sit there during these "visits." I really didn't think it was my place to participate in his life. I've kept in contact with William over the years. Both he and Finn still live in Niagara Falls. However there has never been any bond established between us and of late my phone calls haven't been returned. Its an awkward situation.

The reality of my situation began to set in, and along with that realization came a terrible depression. I was in the midst of a horrible tragedy, a nightmarish struggle. I had no motivation, no energy and I was overwhelmed by hopelessness and despair. I had no future, no self-esteem, no confidence, no friends, no potential. There was no hope. I couldn't get out. I was back in reality, but reality sucked! I had lost everything, friends, my house, my job and my financial security. I faced a huge void – who was I? I was "better," but I felt completely empty. I was out of the delusions but into despair. I realized I was a very ill person with no potential. I would be a burden all my life to those around me. There was no place for me. I was nobody. I was in a black reality. My life as I knew it was completely different. I was no longer the same person that I had always been. On the outside I was the same man, but on the inside everything had changed. I needed to get out. To top it all off, around this time I lost my driver's license. On my doctor's advice, my driving privileges were suspended.

I felt even God wasn't working for me. I no longer had the pressure of my former Jehovah's Witness beliefs to deal with but questioned my new understanding of a personal God. I knew there was a God, but He wasn't working in my life. Maybe He was a tease or possibly a sadist. I later learned that people were praying for me but nobody had experienced what I had gone through. They all said they understood, and today I appreciate their compassion, but others can't really understand. There was no light, no hope, no laughter, no music, not even tears – only empty darkness and despair. These were the longest five years of my life.

When I was discharged from the hospital and went home to live with my parents I had nothing to do. I walked around the neighborhood or paced in the house and drank tea. I craved change. There were days when I even thought of going back to the hospital I hated. At least there was some excitement there. At home the days were so long and identical. I would go over my past; if only I had studied harder, or if I was smarter. I couldn't sleep. My mind went over and over the smallest details. I was often angry. Lying in bed, little things would drive me nuts, like the sound of my Dad clipping his nails in the bathroom.

Mole hills became mountains. There were six billion people in the world. All could cope except me. Why? What was wrong with me? Why couldn't I manage when everyone else could? What I didn't realize at the time was that I was not alone. There are many people who suffer from mental illness every day, I just didn't know it. At times I felt God owed me. After all, I had sacrificed myself for Him at the streetlight.

Cassie came to visit me one time at my parents' house. I asked her to go to dinner with me where I told her about my delusions. I told her I wasn't sick, wasn't crazy. I implored her to believe there was something supernatural going on, trying to convince her it was true. She was shocked at what I told her and asked me where she fit in. Later I learned she went to school in London. I tried to get hold of her but lost touch. She gradually faded from my life. She may have felt guilty, that it was her fault I got Finn pregnant. She wanted to be out of the picture.

Dave Kendrick

Side effects of Bill's medication manifested as sudden jerks and spasms. During church these jerks and spasms sometimes shook the whole pew but the congregation was accepting of this and of Bill.

It was in this period that I had my one and only suicide attempt. I was severely depressed and hated life. The only possible way to escape was to just not exist. This was the only solution I could see. Fifty percent of people with schizophrenia attempt suicide – 10 percent succeed. I tried once. There was so much pain and hurt and I wanted it all to end. I had a bottle of sleeping pills prescribed for my insomnia and one afternoon when Mom was out and Dad was at bingo, I downed the whole bottle. I wrote a note, indicating I saw nothing but darkness for myself. I woke up the next day in the psych ward of the hospital. Ironically that was the very day I was to go to a hearing to get my driver's license returned. My Dad said I was in a "fine mess." Dad had found me a couple of hours after I took the pills and when he couldn't wake me, called the Fort Erie hospital. They pumped out my stomach and gave me a charcoal treatment. I was transferred to hospital in Niagara and woke up later.

May 30, 1988 – Dr. Mitchell

- *Suicide attempt, curt suicide note, took 10 Mandrax capsules, taken to hospital*
- *Has been taking several medicines, been attending day care programme since last discharge.*

May 31, 1988 – Dr. Mitchell

- *Transferred to hospital, drowsy but denies feeling so, distraught, dejected, depressed/*
- *Dr. Mitchell says because of relapse long term prognosis "must be guarded."*
- *In letter to Dr. Kratka, Dr. Mitchell says symptoms are of a negative type, lack of drive, interest, enthusiasm, apathy, low self-confidence. Feels Bill continues to show symptoms of mental illness despite extensive treatment, retains "disabling residual features of mental disorder," adding this time Bill is totally disabled.*
- *Physical exam – Okay*
- *Begins expressing optimism about future*
- *Advised to continue medication, return for follow-up.*

June 3, 1988 – Dr. Mitchell

- *Discharged from hospital*

Hospital PROGRESS NOTES

June 3, 1988

Bill will be discharged today. The past several days he has been denying strongly any thoughts of harming himself. He is concerned about his future but he seems to be a bit more hopeful. One option he will explore is to move to St. Catharines and live in one of the CMHC housing projects while attending Brock University. He is quite rational and appropriate. He is to continue with Norporamin in a dose of 50 mgm. b.i.d., Cogentin, 2 mgm. o.d. and Fluanxol, 30 mgm. i.m. every two weeks.

I was assigned a new counselor, Angela, who came to see me. She said, "You really did something serious this time, but cognitively you're okay." She told me patients were often really screwed up by a suicide attempt, but surprisingly I was fine. The doctor that pumped out my stomach apparently said the same thing – I was strong.

Angela became my main counselor. I saw her about every two weeks. I also went to group therapy every day. I participated from time to time, when I felt like it, and enjoyed it to an extent. I was often unkempt and not cleaned up in these days. I didn't care. I met others, made a few friends and got to know some of them. I saw their skills and abilities, and while encouraging them, thought of myself as nothing.

At home I spent a lot of time pacing but now I had something to look forward to, my meetings with Angela. They were always positive things and I was excited about these as each one came around. Then I would have the meeting, nothing would happen, nothing would change and I would conclude that reality sucks! I would get up, go out and shut the door behind me. Nothing had changed, all was the same. This cycle went on week after week and my hopes dwindled as my depression deepened. It seemed like I was getting nowhere. I would never be normal again.

I kept going back to Angela, telling her "I don't like my life, there must be something better." I sometimes recalled the past and saw it as good. I hoped for quick progress. Angela would say, "You don't understand your illness – how sick you really are." I wanted a better life, but at the same time didn't think a better life existed or was possible - at least not for me. It was impossible to see beyond the grayness of my day-to-day problems. I was depressed thinking I didn't have a future and my parents would have to take care of me for the rest of my life. I'd be a burden on them forever. I saw how my brother Jack lived, alone, friendless and poor and it was frightening and depressing to think about living the same lifestyle. As I began to understand my own illness to some extent, my respect for my Mom grew during this period since I understood a bit of what she had been going through all her life. We had never said Mom was having a manic depressive episode or that she had bipolar mood disorder. We just said she was sick. Back then I believed she was sick because she was weak.

At one time I had crime fantasies. I thought I'd be better off if I committed a crime and went to jail. No one would have to take care of me and there would be no high expectations. If I were locked up for committing a crime, there would at least be a clear, if not pleasant, existence. To some extent I understood people killing other people. Maybe they were striving for recognition or purpose. At one point I even looked into getting a gun and a license. I went to Canadian Tire to look for a gun. I can still picture the shiny rifles on the wall, but I didn't know if I needed a license or not. I was going to ask them where I had to go and what to do, but I chickened out and left. I probably wouldn't have known how to use a gun anyway, or would have done something silly like shoot myself in the foot. I tried to think of other ways to commit a crime. If I had been smart enough to build a nuclear bomb, I would have.

Someone who has schizophrenia needs social skills and an understanding of their strengths to deal with the illness. With medicine and personal strength, a person would be able to pick up his or her life when stabilized. However, it's at this point in the illness that personal strength is at its lowest. During this period I experienced many contradictory feelings. At some deep level of self, I knew I had potential while my daily life was filled with frustrations, negativity and failure. In time Angela filled out the paperwork for me to go to a group home in Welland. She realized clearly my need for socialization with other people. But I hated the group home. The people there were "mentally ill." They weren't like me. I was just dealing with my symptoms. This place was a dirty mess. It wasn't for me. I felt very frustrated about being there and never felt like it was where I belonged. One day I walked in on a guy spitting in the kitchen sink and it angered me because that's where we washed our dishes. Another guy named Darcy continually wrote notes on a pad, possibly trying to remember or make some sense of his life. I once overheard the staff talking about me. They said, "Bill is going to be the role model of the house." They saw me as high functioning and not psychotic. I hated that. I had no future, all was negative for me. I knew I didn't belong there because I thought I had better potential. I had a son I couldn't provide for, and I was a role model for failure. I recall going to events at William's mother's house, and overhearing comments from others that I had no job. I was distraught and disabled. It was a mess. I had no life. It was too far to jump to reach opportunity. I alternated between angry despair and a persistent spark of belief in my own potential. I needed smaller steps. I didn't stay in the group home very long, just a few weeks. I soon moved back into my parent's house.

I remember in one of our sessions Angela, who was Irish, told me a story of when she was a young girl in Ireland. She rode her bike to school and she had a pet crow that would come to her and ride on the handlebars of her bike. I thought this was amazing. I also found it a little strange. Angela's daughter got very sick with cancer of the nose. She was on her deathbed, but suddenly recovered. It was like a healing. Again, this was an incredible thing to me. Angela had a very strong effect on me even though I didn't know it at the time. She was a great person with strong professional abilities and understanding in an era when very little was known of my illness. I must attribute much of my recovery to her efforts and patient work with me. Some time ago I was sad to learn she died of a brain tumor.

Psychiatry is a relatively young field. In the 1950s there was no understanding of mental illness. People were warehoused or perhaps had lobotomies performed. They were institutionalized for life. Some also had physical problems and often had to be anesthetized to prevent violence. Doctors began noticing people with psychoses would be well for a while after an operation. They thought this was the result of the anesthetics. So a "family" of tranquilizing drugs in the 50's and 60's was developed to help ill patients. These stopped the symptoms of mental illnesses but left the people zombie-like. It wasn't until 1994 that the whole field of neuroleptics began with the development of many new medications. Not all work well. Each individual has to discover the best combinations, mainly through trial and error. Today medication is the foundation of getting back into reality.

The person who had perhaps the greatest impact on my long road to recovery was my friend Dave Kendrick. He was a good guy. Right from the beginning he visited me every night I was in the hospital. He was the most patient person and seemed to dedicate his life to seeing me recover. It was most amazing. He would arrive around 6 pm and always wore an old hockey jacket that he would take off and hang on the chair in my room. I always worried that it would get stolen, but Dave wasn't concerned. During my times of psychosis I thought Dave had special knowledge and powers. He would walk endlessly with me as I paced the halls. When I moaned, "I have no future" Dave would respond, "You have a bright future." I often went to Dave's house on weekends. We had many bible studies together. During my times out of the hospital Dave took me to the Sherkston Brethern In Christ church. I felt relieved and comfortable and there was good music there. At one point in a preacher's message he gave a call to be saved. I prayed and accepted Christ. Dave very patiently and slowly explained things to me, particularly when I raised details of the Jehovah's Witness theology. I remember one incident when I had left my shoes at the Kingdom Hall following a meeting there. Of course I thought my shoes were magical. One of the Jehovah's Winness guys, Dan Hanuska, brought my shoes to me. Dave was there too and I saw this as a confrontation of good versus evil. The JWs knew Dave as he accused them of spreading "false doctrine." My experience with the Jehovah's Witnesses was a stressor in my life, along with Finn's pregnancy. For me the doctrine added stress. I felt I had to perform at a high level. There were always more meetings to attend, more witnessing to do. But incredibly, it was while I was involved with the Jehovah's Witnesses that I first started my journey toward God with the reading of "Creation vs. Evolution." I also instinctively knew that God was good. I never got turned off to religion, never developed bitterness toward God.

Years later Dave got a form of leukemia and after a variety of treatments, passed away. At his funeral, I had the honor of bringing part of the eulogy.

Eulogy exerpts

"Dave was a devout Christian. He searched the scriptures and studied doctrine and knew why he believed. He had a deep faith. When I was hospitalized with my mental breakdown 16 years ago, I was lying in bed sleeping. When I woke the first person I saw was Dave. He was praying silently for me. Dave took me under his wing, he became my friend. He introduced me to friends, some of whom I still have today. Later in my recovery he'd drive me home and I'd fall asleep in his car. One time he wanted to cut down a tree in his yard. He decided to rent a chainsaw at Pen Rentals. Dave drove very slow. We went to the rental place, got the saw, got gas and drove all the way back out to Ridgeway. It took forever for the trip. When we tried to use the saw we realized it was dull. I thought I'd be very angry at this but Dave said we'd just go back to Pen Rentals and get them to sharpen the saw. It took him about 40 minutes for the drive. I don't know what time he woke up to go to work, it took him so long to do anything. But Dave had special timing, he realized everything happened for a reason.

He would walk with me every night as I paced in the Niagara Falls hospital, every single night. I was always disturbed and angry, Dave was so faithful! I remember saying, "What does my future hold?" Dave said, "Bill, you have a bright future." Dave was always there for me.

I know Dave is in eternity. He's started his way in eternity. I envy him sometimes, he's there, he knows what its about, he's seeing things. Dave's future is bright too. When we get to eternity, if Dave is going as slow through eternity as he drove, when we get there we'll catch up to him."

In Dave's own language it was a zinger. People applauded my eulogy. Leonard Chester, the pastor of the church, said he'd never seen people clap at a funeral before.

Dave spent a lot of time with me. He even invited me to vacation with his family at their family cottage. I remember Dave was very hurt by my suicide attempt. He couldn't understand why. I was loved by him, his family and God! Why would I try to end my life? But I couldn't see God's love. If God loved me, I thought I wouldn't be in this situation. I went to lots of activities with Dave's family and lots of bible studies. The calming influence of Dave's consistent companionship brought me through this period of my life. I remember his low, quiet voice and his even-tempered approach to life.

During these long, slow, agonizing years I was living with my parents and the symptoms of my illness were controlled by medication. However, I was dealing with my lack of motivation, energy and depression. In this state I found myself thinking all the time, "If only I had studied or done something differently, if Mom had a different education or Dad had a different career." I realized the awful truth of the saying "if things don't change, they remain the same"! It drove me insane that Dad did the same meaningless things day after day. He went to bingo every day, watched the same TV shows, and played endless card games. There was no life to it all. The years dragged by, one excruciating day at a time. I wasn't doing anything; I wasn't exercising or going anywhere. I ate a lot, it was a comfort thing. I ate just about anything. My weight slowly crept up to 260 pounds, but I had no motivation or desire to do anything about it. One time someone asked my Dad about my appetite. He replied, "He certainly hasn't lost that." My mom would be out shovelling the snow, and my brother Tom would yell at me for not helping her at her age. He was the athletic one and couldn't understand how I could sit back and watch Mom working, or why I wouldn't go to the gym and become the next Arnold Schwarzenegger. I hated my situation. It was a bitter pill. I hated this, and I began to hate myself. I desperately had to find a spark.

One of my worries at this time was that I might become like my brother Jack. He had made my childhood unpleasant. His attitude was always negative in the house. I became aware I was becoming like him. Dad told me I was lucky to have a home, he had told Jack he couldn't come back once he was out of the house. Jack was always "a problem" teamed up with an attitude. He was always in trouble. Mom called him "the other one." He was the author of his own difficulties. He was his own worst enemy. I was acutely aware that I was going down a very similar road.

In mid 1988 I spent much of my days in bed. I'd go to bed at 6pm and just lie there. It was a very hot summer and we had no air conditioning. I got irritated and took my mattress down to the basement. I lay there thinking, "How could I be in this spot?" The dark, damp basement in the lowest part of the house seemed to fit my mental condition perfectly.

I was continually focused on myself. There was nothing else but my sorrow and misery. I wasn't nice to be around so people stayed away from me. They weren't sure what to say to me anyway. It was all meaningless. Dad just watched TV. It drove me crazy but I was there on the couch too, right alongside him. Mom wanted Dad to talk to me but poor Dad didn't know what to say. He'd escape to bingo in the afternoons. Eventually I began babysitting for my sister who had triplets. I went with Mom and drank tea all day. From time to time Dad would take me for a drive to Chippawa, a few kilometers down the beautiful Niagara

Parkway. We wouldn't talk much on these drives, just look out the car windows at the river flowing toward Niagara Falls.

Little details about that time still stand out it my mind. We didn't have a shower in the house –we had to take baths. I felt like I never got clean in the bath. Today I certainly appreciate showers. If anyone has a loved one with a mental illness, be sure to have a shower in the house. They will feel better being clean.

Lying in bed at 6pm I wanted the world to end. I often prayed for Jesus to come that night. There was no hope for the future. I looked at my brother Jack who lived in a group home. I thought I'd become just like the person I hated the most. Once again I thought, "If things don't change they'll stay the same." I hated my "same."

Sometimes I'd visit Mr. and Mrs. Yando, an elderly couple on our street. I'd have tea with them a couple of times a week. I could always have tea with Mom too. I often plagued my parents with the common "What can I do?" complaint. I tried a lawn service business, a small engine repair business. I was part of N-TEC for a while, a local association that tried to find employment for challenged people. Later I had training with N-TEC.

N-TEC October 25, 1989

> *Dear Dr. Mitchell,*
>
> *I am writing to inform you Bill MacPhee attended our program for one day in the Custodial Services Department. He felt too anxious to continue.*
>
> *In speaking with his supervisor, Bill worked well on his first day. He worked efficiently and followed instructions*

without hesitation. His supervisor saw potential for Bill in this line of work.

Bill called me this morning to state he would not return to N-TEC due to several anxiety attacks he experienced yesterday. Bill was counseled to try another day and was reinforced for his efforts yesterday. Bill stated he had made up his mind and he was not returning. It was left open for Bill to call me if he should reconsider his position.

Yours Sincerely

Even in my state of mind at that point, I saw much better potential for myself than pushing dust around a factory. Today I see some humor in this, as I run my own media company.

CHAPTER 8

TURNING POINT

At this time I was also having regular talks with Dr. Mitchell at the Niagara Falls hospital. I was involved in church activities but there was little real meaning to them. I recall seeing an ad in the paper for a job at Marineland, an amusement park and aquarium in Niagara Falls. They were looking for a trainer apprentice to work with dolphins and whales. I thought to myself, "I can do this, I have my diving certificate. I swam with dolphins in the South China Sea." I applied, went for an interview and was on the short list for the job. I thought – "This is it, it's perfect." They came back to me asking for references and I put down Bill Western, the brother of a trainer who worked at Marineland. I knew him from the underwater recovery unit years before. This was probably a bad move – I didn't get the job! I was furious – at everybody and at God. "What kind of God are you?" I thought. "You give me hope, You tease me, by doing this to me. You set me up, then there's no job." I turned off God and was very angry, and very discouraged for a period of time.

Of course now I see I would still be there feeding dolphins if things hadn't worked out as they did.

My grade seven teacher, Sister Saleema told me if I didn't learn to write properly, I wouldn't amount to anything. Seemingly out of the blue I said to myself, "I'm going to prove I can do something." I contacted the Fort Erie Literacy Council and told them I wanted to improve my penmanship. Martha Mason called me. She was the Executive

Director of Big Brothers and Big Sisters, and a volunteer with the Literacy Council. She came over to see me, but for this visit I had to clean up, wash my hair and shave. This was a big step for me. Martha worked with me weekly on penmanship exercises. She learned a lot about schizophrenia from me but sadly I didn't learn much penmanship from her. However, she was interested in me, perhaps seeing some potential. She suggested I sign up at Niagara College, and told me she would drive me there. So now I had a problem: I had to get cleaned up and dressed on a regular basis. I went ahead and signed up, for a photography course. After all I had the company of a woman. This was a great incentive. I went to school every Thursday. I even bought a camera and went on field trips. But before long I found myself just going through the motions. There was no joy in it. My enthusiasm evaporated in a short time. I was just filling in time. This would not be my future.

One night Martha called me to say one of the local Boy Scout troupes needed a treasurer, would I be interested? I thought to myself, "My god, I'll have to wash and clean up every day." Still, I went to their next meeting, became their treasurer and began to develop a new circle of friends. Little did I know at the time, this would prove to be the turning point in my life and these small incremental steps would lead me back to health.

I began to hang around with Peter Johnson, Martha's husband, and her children, playing racquetball and other activities with their family. I helped with the Scouts' apple day fundraiser, Kub Kar races, and camp-outs. I now had true friends. These people accepted me for who I was and not what I had. School, Scouts, penmanship, squash and racquetball – I was having lots of fun and building a life.

It soon came to my attention that since all my new friends worked, I needed to work also. I had tried before at Greater Canada Colour, Barney Printing in Woodstock, and other places. I took the John Howard Society Social Program and tried N-TEC – a rehab place. I bought a cell phone and took grocery orders for people. I then did their shopping for them. I tried a landscaping business, buying a trailer and lawn mowers. I raked leaves and did other odd jobs, but this only lasted a day or two. Through the John Howard Society I became a driver for people in wheelchairs. I took a Niagara College Social Studies course. Each of these jobs gradually rebuilt my personal sense of value.

Through it all I still needed that spark that I was looking for – some kind of business that matched my personality.

I called Vaughn Gibbons at Gibbons Construction and told him I was looking for a job. I knew Vaughn from church. He told he would need a flagman in a couple of weeks. Incredibly I did this for a whole winter, standing in the freezing cold directing busy traffic at construction sites. The irony of my initial delusions and breakdown on a busy highway in freezing February weather a few years prior is still not lost on me today. At this time I was living on my own again in a small cottage near members of my very supportive church family. I joined Nutra System, started losing weight and was soon in good shape. But I hated the work. The days were long, damp, cold, and repetitive. I was still convinced God has a much bigger plan for me.

I went to hear bands at the band shell in a park near the Old Fort Erie. I went to the library to read the postings on the bulletin boards. I loved reading bulletin boards. I became interested in municipal politics and started attending town council meetings at the library. I sat through many of these sessions. My long days of depression and darkness seemed to be behind me. I regularly took my medication and my illness was kept under control.

I still carried an entrepreneurial spirit inside me and one day while browsing the library shelves. Came across the book "101 Ways to Start a Business Without Any Capital." As I started to read it I came across a chapter about a woman who, before the advent of VCRs watched soap operas every day. She decided to write up a newsletter on the soaps to recap the storylines. Then she sold the newsletter to her friends who weren't able to watch. I thought this was an amazing idea and she must have been an amazing person to have thought of it. At that moment a light bulb flashed in my head, "I can do this on schizophrenia." This was an opportunity, my moment. Why not do the same thing for people with schizophrenia by means of a magazine?

This became my dream, my purpose, my goal, and my mission. I felt hope for the first time in so many years. My existence had meaning again. I thought my heart was going to burst. People with mental illness battle poor confidence and poor self-esteem. They feel like failures and just want to be left alone. Its extremely difficult to keep picking yourself up and trying again with the feeling there is no meaningful place left and no future ahead. Success requires persistence. It's like Thomas Edison who tried many components for the element for the light bulb before discovering the right one or Stephen King who wrote hundreds of stories and books before one was published.

For me it was all about believing. There's always a way with God. With the discovery of my purpose I became a hound dog with my goal. I knew I had to go slow or people would think this was just another of my crazy ideas. Dave Kendrick's wife, Glennis, even remarked, "How grandiose can you get?" But I knew I had something. There was no other publication like it and I had a real vision of what this magazine would be like. I knew I needed a marketing plan so I devised a survey to circulate to people with schizophrenia. At the time, there were forty chapters of the Schizophrenia Society around Ontario so I sent the survey to all of them and their members, about three hundred surveys. The response rate was exactly 10% which was a fantastic response (the expected response rate to surveys is about 5%). A friend of mine who received the survey tells me she still remembers the day she got it and how she thought nothing would ever come of it.

I also enrolled in Niagara College's "How To Start a Small Business" course. During my time in this course I got to know John Seemas, manager of Crabtree Publishing. John is still a great friend today.

I discovered that one of my best skills is networking. It comes very naturally for me and I have no hesitation to call somebody and ask for whatever I need. The business first operated out of my parents' basement. My first editor, Tanya V. said she couldn't believe me. "He phones people and they phone him back."

I went to the Small Business Club of Niagara. I also went to the Enterprise Store in St. Catharines. It was a free course offered by the government. All you needed was an idea and a dream. I certainly had those. There were fifteen of us in the course. We networked. One day I called Phyllis Barnett, editor of the local newspaper, The Times, in Fort Erie. She was also a journalism teacher at Niagara College. I went to see her, looking for a writer to work with me. She assigned me a student, Samantha who became my personal assistant. I took her to the Enterprise Store and the other participants marvelled that "Bill has his own private secretary."

I knew I needed a business plan so I went to the Brock University consulting department in St. Catharines to get one put together for me. This was my first real plan.

There was just one problem. I had no money! Banks wouldn't touch me! I went to the Business Development Corporation (BDC) in Fort Erie, showed them my plan and made an application. They offered me a loan of $60,000 on the condition that my father would guarantee it. Dad warned me, "Don't get your hopes up" but I knew I had a winner. He must have known it too because he mortgaged his house in order for me to get the loan. His words were, "If you don't go for it the rest of your life you'll wonder what would have happened if..." I felt appreciative.

Dad knew I was working hard. He would have done anything for me, you know.

I set up shop in the basement of my parents' house. I incorporated in March 1994 and in June 1994 I published our first "teaser issue." It was eight pages. I called it Schizophrenia Digest. We had free stories, a freelance editor, a graphic designer and no computer skills. I had gotten a good graphic designer in Diane Coderre. She was an old-school graphic designer, who was used to manually creating layouts, not like the graphic designers we have today who do everything on a computer. The first layout she did for me was the first time she ever designed something on a computer.

I had a goal, a dream and the first small steps were underway. And I was still on Canada Pension Plan disability. Years later I called to cancel this. They were very surprised that I had my own business and was working. But ironically there was no process to get a person off disability. They told me to send in some paperwork, there were a few calls back and forth and finally I got a letter from them saying I was no longer eligible.

And then I had what was probably the second of the happiest moments in my life to that point. The first was landing my first diving job with Seatek International in the South China Sea, this one was selling my first ad in my magazine to Bristol-Meyers Squib, a pharmaceutical company that produced a medication for schizophrenia. Keep in mind I was very naïve at this point. I didn't know much of what I was doing. Publishing is a tough business. Patty Tardiff said, "If there's a business that will fail, it will be this one." Phyliss Barnett and the board of the BDC got the first sample of the magazine and they were all were very surprised. Their mouths just dropped. I sold one-year subscriptions for $19.95. But I still needed more money to continue. Sixty thousand dollars wasn't much, even in those days. So I had an idea – I would offer two-year subscriptions at double the cost. This would potentially double my immediate revenue. I hired a blind fellow figuring he'd be good at cold calls. I also took on a salesperson and found out later he was mentally ill with depression.

But I had the drive, the excitement, driven to run by the skin of my teeth. At the beginning I had a "Christian Corner" in the magazine. It was a small space for views of the illness from a Christian perspective and other comments. An Islamic guy called me and questioned this. He said nobody would advertise and the magazine wouldn't last because of the "Christian Corner." Now when I speak, it's clear and all know I'm a Christian.

I never thought I'd be speaking, it wasn't ever in the plan. I was on the Board of Gateway Housing and the president asked me to speak at the AGM. I prepared a speech feeling like I was inspired. I believe now I truly was. That first talk I gave at that meeting is basically the same one I deliver today. It's been enhanced and embellished some but it's the same one. I remember telling God, "You have to do this, I don't know how." To this day I don't know how. It isn't easy but somehow I manage.

I look back at the first incident of my illness. God was starting something. I simply responded with prayer. I feel very thankful. My spiritual life is extremely important to me and our family. There is no doubt God wants my success, he's leading me each step. Some powerful things I learned have come from the well-known preacher Charles Stanley. He says God is for us. It's not the "prosperity gospel" but there are natural principles and with these we have a better shot at success. I've lived it. I recall being with my close friend Dave Kendrick and visiting one of his friends. The friend happened to say "The Lord is faithful." I remember thinking, "That's easy for him to say, what about me?" I now have the gift of faith, I have no doubts about what God is doing in my life. The Roman centurion in the Bible with the ill slave had faith. He sent his servant to Jesus to ask him to heal the man and to also say he wasn't worthy to have Jesus come to his house. Jesus comment was that he'd not seen that type of faith in Judea! I see myself like that centurion.

Whatever came up, we always got through it, there was always a way. This is a complete reversal from those days of horror when I was suicidal and in a very dark place. I remember once in the very early days of the business plan I was making calls to marketing firms with my idea. I called one guy, then later went to bed. The next morning I called the guy back and told him my idea …again. He said, "We talked yesterday, we had the exact same conversation." I felt so stupid I got into my bed and pulled the covers over my head for three days. I was very fragile then, today I feel I'm strong in my faith in God.

CHAPTER 9
AILEEN

In 1994 my business was off the ground and going well. What I lacked personally was a relationship with someone. Like most of us, I wanted to be loved. I tried a Christian dating organization in St. Catharines and was put in touch with a girl whom I wrote to a few times. In one of my letters I told her of my illness. She wrote back to me that she could never have anything to do with someone with my illness because her mother had suffered through it for many years. Of course I felt down as a result of this.

I went on my computer and searched a "mail order bride" site. Sunshine International came up. I sent them the required $60 and a package came back in two weeks. There were pictures, biographies, addresses and telephone numbers of hundreds of Asian women! I had two criteria for a relationship – she had to be a Christian and she needed to be attractive. I checked off eighty-two women from the site and drafted a form letter to send to them. However, I had a problem – Asian women (whom I've always found attractive) are generally petite and I was 260 pounds! I did the "math" and there was no equal sign to be found! So I drove all over Fort Erie and found a very large tree on Lakeshore Road. I then had a photographer take my picture next to this tree in the hope of making me look thinner! I sent out my letters, complete with picture. When I did so, I pointed to Aileen's picture and said. "I hope she writes back" and she did!

She was working as a nanny in Singapore and we started writing. She knew about Sunshine International, had held their paperwork for a long time, never filling it in until shortly before I checked the site. There was lots of interest in Aileen on the website, but none made the trip to Singapore.

I have two good friends, Peter and Elizabeth Johnson, who do a lot of travelling. One of their trips at this time was to the east, including Singapore. Elizabeth said she would look up Aileen and go to dinner with her. She actually carried through with this and reported to me that Aileen was a great person and she looked like she was sixteen.

Aileen

Bill was very slow in his replies to me, there were actually only two or three letters during that year. In February of 1998 Bill came to Singapore to visit me. He stayed for three weeks, however we only saw each other two or three times. My job as a nanny restricted my time off. I must have made an impression because to my surprise Bill proposed to me before he left.

Bill

On our first date Aileen had to take the subway to my hotel. She was two agonizing hours late! When she arrived she apologized profusely and when we turned to walk, she took my arm. I thought I'd arrived in heaven. I remember we had great conversations together, even though we were very new to each other. One particularly funny incident occurred when we were talking about the Singapore zoo. Aileen was listing the animals by name, lions, tigers, bears and hippopothamusses. I wondered about this last animal and we went back and forth with lots of laughter till I got her to realize it was hippopotamus!

It came closer to the end of my stay in Singapore so I finally brought up the details of my illness. I was quite nervous about this from the reaction of the other girl in St. Catharines. Aileen didn't know anything about this illness so I gave her a few of my magazines I had published. She said she would talk this over with her sister Brenda who was a nurse. Brenda was very positive, telling Aileen that with medication and support, people with schizophrenia are fine. Aileen relayed her confidence back to me. I remember thinking here was somebody in the Third World and she was willing to take a chance on me.

I proposed to Aileen in McDonalds. She said she would think about it but we went shopping for rings anyway.

Aileen

Bill came prepared with a letter from his pastor, Leonard Chester, saying that he was a strong Christian. I had been praying to find the right person for my life. I was reassured that he was the right one for me, he even talked about his faith openly.

So – when he proposed, I said "yes," confident that God had answered my prayers.

Bill

I came back to Canada while Aileen made plans for our wedding. It was scheduled for August 1998 in the Philippines. I called Aileen every Wednesday to see how arrangements were going, and, of course to chat with her. I knew I needed my own house, since I was still living with my parents. There was a house for sale beside my parents' home on Ellen Street. It had been on the market for a couple of years. I managed to purchase this house for the sum of $50,000.

Aileen

My mother raised four girls by herself. She was always working to raise us. When she met Bill the first time she approved of him. I had let her read Bill's letters to me, she knew Bill would look after me. She wasn't worried about me going all the way to Canada. Mom trusted God in all this. Her confident words to me were, "I'll pray for you."

When Bill came over for our wedding he didn't know of all the arrangements necessary for him to marry overseas. He needed a document in the Philippines and hadn't gotten the letter from the Canadian embassy in time. We were worried all our plans might have to be cancelled but we flew to Manila to get the document. To our immense relief we ended up getting it just three days before the wedding.

Our wedding went smoothly. Bill's friend Peter Johnson came over to be his best man. We had over 100 people there and all had a great time. We were married in an outside, landscaped garden – the "Garden Oasis" in Davao. It was beautiful. The reception was in a big restaurant right in the garden. We honeymooned in Paradise Island, a beautiful resort on the other side of our island.

Bill

Immediately after this I had to return to Canada – without my new bride. From this point in time it took thirteen months to navigate the Canadian Immigration system and get Aileen to Canada!

Aileen

In October of 1999 I came to Canada. I flew the long sixteen hour trip by myself. I remember at around 8pm the plane arrived at the airport in

Toronto. After lots of paperwork, documents and offices I came out the door of the airport. Bill was right in front of me. We hugged for a long time. We moved into Bill's house on Ellen St and for two weeks I could hardly get out of bed. I was jet-lagged, exhausted and freezing, October in Canada.

For about two months I just stayed at home. People were very nice to me, especially the church people. We lived on Ellen St. for four years, then moved to our new home in Fort Erie.

I soon got going and in February of 2000 I went to adult classes at Fort Erie Secondary School for computers. Under the exceptional teaching of John Kohinski I learned computers for the first time. I learned Word, Excel, Power Point and the Internet, got good grades and congratulations from the principal. While I was doing this Bill was operating his office on Jarvis St. His subscription manager decided to resign so at the same time as I was taking computer courses at school, I was trained by our outgoing manager to handle all the subscription details in our data base. I took over the position of subscription manager and have been doing that for the last twelve years. There's been a lot of computer learning!

During 2000 I also enrolled in a driver's course with Young Drivers of Canada to get my license. In September I finally took the test and passed. I now officially could drive. Early in 2001 I went to Niagara College to study bookkeeping. This was all part of our plan. I wanted to help Bill and be part of his business. Later Bill's bookkeeper left the company so I took over that job too.

In May of 2002 our son Dwight came along. I didn't take any maternity leave but went back to work almost immediately. I didn't want to stop working. At the same time I processed paperwork for my sister Brenda to come to Canada so she could look after our son. Brenda arrived in 2003. She watched Dwight while I worked. In 2004 Hannah, our daughter came into our family. Brenda now had her hands full with a niece and nephew while I worked full time.

CHAPTER 10

PERSPECTIVE

As I look back over the years and recall the many people who were part of my life and instrumental in my journey through the darkness of my illness to the incredible life I have with my family and friends today, I must make special reference to the tireless professionalism and patience of Dr. Wallace Mitchell. From the first days of my illness through countless treatments, interviews, medications, setbacks and a few victories he was instrumental in my recovery. There wasn't a lot known about schizophrenia twenty-five years ago and Dr. Mitchell often had little to go on to deal with me. His work was extraordinary at every step. I include the text of a letter I sent him in the early years of my recovery and his encouraging, polite reply.

Dr. Mitchell:

Hi, Doc this is Bill MacPhee you have treated me on and off for the last four years. I am just writing you, to thank you for your time and professionalism. It has taken four years but I am doing very well, especially the last year.

Since October I have been enrolled in a job re-entry program called touchstone training centre. It has brought my motivation up as well as my self-esteem. I am now working in the construction field and am doing very well. I have plans in the future of building a house and getting some of my social status back, the future seems to be getting brighter.

I know you are a very busy man so I won't keep you long, I just want to encourage you and tell you to have patience and make you aware that even the worst cases of mental illnesses can come out with some degree of certain success. You see so much of society's imperfections and troubled but all deserve love and compassion. Mental illness and depression are an awful sort of hell and only God knows why he puts us through it. I hope all is well with you and ask that you keep up the good work and please don't become discouraged. May God bless you.

Yours Sincerely

William MacPhee

Dear Bill,

It was nice to receive your letter and learn that you have come out of your slump and have become involved in the world around you.

Thank you for your kind words.

Best wishes for the future.

Yours Sincerely

Wallace M. Mitchell

My other dear friend was Dave Kendrick. He was a devoted Christian friend who gave of his time in countless hours of sitting and walking with me through every dark path. He was selfless in his determination to see me recover. I often wondered what motivated Dave. I can only conclude it was the love of God deep within him. He was a Godly man. In all likelihood I owe my life to him. Sadly he passed away some years ago as I alluded to earlier. For the rest of my life I will remember his pleasant manner and dedication.

I have often found myself burnt out, particularly from travelling. I sit in front of my computer and nothing comes. A balance is important, particularly with family. Lots of people say "family comes first." I feel this is an overused cliché. I wouldn't say I use that motto. But I do book my time, including flexibility in my schedule. For instance I pick my kids up at their school bus regularly and go to my son's important soccer games. Our business is our livelihood, for our quality of life. I have to work hard. People who succeed have often come from nothing. It's also true that children whose parents were entrepreneurs and failed are often very successful, having seen what their parents did wrong.

FACTS ABOUT SCHIZOPHRENIA

WHAT IT IS

Schizophrenia is a biologically based brain disease that affects approximately 1 percent of the population worldwide, in all cultures and countries, with about equal numbers of men and women. It usually strikes in the late teenage and early adult years, most commonly between 15 and 25 years of age in men and between 25 and 35 years in women.

Schizophrenia is a form of psychotic disorder, which means it can cause people to have difficulty interpreting reality. Individuals develop a marked change in their thinking, perceptions, and behavior.

WHAT IT ISN'T

Schizophrenia has nothing to do with "split personality" or "multiple personality" (now called dissociative disorder).

SYMPTOMS

"Positive" symptoms – disturbances that are added to someone's personality – include hallucinations (false sensations), delusions (false beliefs), disorganized thinking and speech, and agitation and movement disorders.

"Negative" symptoms – capabilities that are lost – include lack of drive or initiative, apathy, social withdrawal, and flat affect (emotional unresponsiveness). People who have schizophrenia may experience some, all, or a combination of these symptoms.

According to the DSM-IV (Diagnostic and Statistical Manual of Mental Disorders, Fourth Edition, Text Revision, American Psychiatric Publishing), one must have associated symptoms for at least six months to be diagnosed as having schizophrenia.

CAUSES

Schizophrenia is believed to occur as a result of a disturbance in the development of the brain. It is currently thought that this occurs as a result of genetic factors, although environmental factors may also play a role. As is the case for many other medical illnesses, the illness appears to occur many years after the genetic factors and underlying developmental changes have been expressed.

Schizophrenia is not caused by psychological conflicts or stress or drug use. Sometimes these factors seem to be important in precipitating an acute episode of illness, but this is only believed to occur in individuals who are otherwise predisposed to develop schizophrenia. Recent studies have suggested that individuals with a genetic vulnerability who use illicit drugs may increase their chances of developing schizophrenia.

TREATMENT

There is no cure for schizophrenia; however, medications have been proven to be effective for many of the symptoms. With proper medication, some people will have complete resolution of all their symptoms. Hallucinations, paranoia and delusions often improve over a number of weeks. Social withdrawal and apathy will also improve, but sometimes to a lesser extent than these other symptoms.

Medications available to date are not perfect. They can have side effects, some of which can be long lasting. Once the symptoms of schizophrenia are improved with medications, it is almost always the case that medications will be needed for a long period of time, as the risk of becoming ill again after discontinuing medications is extremely high.

Talk therapies and support groups are also important in helping people adjust to their illness.

PROGNOSIS

Prior to the introduction of antipsychotic medication, it was presumed that schizophrenia led to a deteriorating course that ultimately ended in chronic hospitalization. Thankfully, this is no longer the case. The prognosis can only get better. New research studies are continuously underway to discover not only the causes behind schizophrenia, but also new and improved treatments.

As a result of new medications, the outlook for people with schizophrenia has greatly improved over the past 30 years. With proper treatment, many people with schizophrenia are able to lead productive lives in the community.

THE HUMAN ECONOMIC TOLL

Schizophrenia affects about 2.4 million Americans and 300,000 Canadians and has a devastating impact on those who suffer from it, as well as their family and friends. Ten percent of people who develop schizophrenia will commit suicide. Schizophrenia is believed to cost the US economy about $65 billion a year in direct and indirect costs.

AUTHOR'S NOTES

As I set out to write Bill Macphee's story I had no idea I'd embarked on a most extraordinary journey. After countless hours spent with Bill, and poring over his notes and documents from years past I realize his life has been a remarkable story of facing impossible difficulties and conquering incredible odds. Bill is a person with a huge inner drive that will not allow him to ever give up, despite circumstances that would defeat most of us. The onset of schizophrenia and his subsequent descent into the hell of deep depression for five long years would have defeated most ordinary people for life. This is the story of a person who would not give up. Bill's extraordinary inner drive, the help of devoted friends, skilled medical professionals and his personal faith in God have brought Bill back from this abyss to a life of remarkable success in his business and family. For Bill it's always been "ledges and thin air... beckoning".

I have come to have great admiration for Bill's clear direction for his own future as well as his commitment to helping others that suffer the effects of mental illnesses of all kinds. In writing Bill's story, I hope others can see all things are possible.